True North
By Randall DeVallance

For information, or to order additional copies, please contact:

Beacon Publishing Group
P.O. Box 41573 Charleston, S.C. 29423
800.817.8480| beaconpublishinggroup.com

Publisher's catalog available by request.

ISBN-13: 978-1-961504-01-1

ISBN-10: 1-961504-01-1

Published in 2023. New York, NY 10001.

First Edition. Printed in the USA.

True North

True North

One

A scream from the front signaled they were almost there. Right on cue the bus began rocking from side to side like a trawler navigating a stormy sea. Salvatore Slocum felt himself falling and made a desperate grab for the handrail. He caught it just in time, fingertips latching onto the metal bar as he hurtled toward the passengers seated to his right.

"Aaaah!" shrieked a woman's voice directly below him. Sal couldn't make out her face. A man of modest stature ("closer to six feet than to five" was as specific as he would get when asked how tall he was), he required every last inch of his person to keep hold of the railing. Raised up on tiptoes, arms extended toward the sky, he rocked gently from side to side like an Evangelical listening to a particularly rousing sermon.

"Get off me, you brute!" said the woman's voice.

"Now, look here," said Sal. He tried tilting his head down to look his complainant in the eyes, but it was no use. Every time he lowered his chin he could feel his fingers begin to slide away from the railing, and would thrust himself upward once more to

1

reestablish his grip. Suspended between floor and handrail, he swayed with the rhythms of the bus like a prize marlin dangling from the end of a hook.

"Aaaah!" shrieked the woman again.

"Now, look here," said Sal. "What's the matter with you?"

"What's the matter with *me*?" said the voice. It sounded so close it seemed to be emanating from his bellybutton. Sal could feel the woman's warm breath on his stomach whenever she spoke. "What's the matter with *me*?"

Sal looked out the window – his only choice, stuck as he was – at the concrete plaza with the cluster of identical, black-glass buildings, each one a perfect cube, creeping toward him through the dawn light. Even without looking he would have known he'd arrived. The bone-rattling vibrations of the bus as it neared his stop were as familiar to him as an old trick knee that started throbbing right before the rains came.

In the middle of an otherwise pristine street, the block in front of his office complex was pockmarked and crumbling, perpetually untouched by the city's repair crews, as if it were hidden from them by some powerful ward. Sal wondered if it had something to do with the sculptures scattered about the plaza, a memorial to the Balkan War of the 1990s. Perhaps a section of bombed-out pavement had been excised from a street in Belgrade and placed here in tribute, he thought, though it was hard to imagine that even NATO could punish a slab of asphalt as comprehensively as the city of Ashburg had managed.

"Yes, you," said Sal. "What is the matter with *you*?"

"*Why I...!*" There came a gagging sound, followed by a sharp exhalation that to Sal sounded like someone blowing into a breathalyzer. "In my day, a young man did not address a lady so!"

Sal had been working for a company called True North for more than a year. By his calculations that meant he had spent at least five-hundred hours of his life riding the bus to and from this grim outskirt of town, a sprawling industrial park full of corporate headquarters and administrative offices protruding from the southwestern corner of Ashburg like a cancerous growth. He had picked the job at random out of the classified section of a free weekly newspaper after his girlfriend, LuAnn (*ex-girlfriend*, he reminded himself) had threatened to leave him if he didn't get off the couch and do something with his life. She had left him anyway, but the job remained. Sal couldn't help feeling he'd been duped somehow.

That first day, huddled up shivering on the streetcorner as the bus hissed to a stop in front of him, he had clambered aboard expecting to have his pick of seats, only to find that the bus was packed. No matter, he thought, he would stand until the crowd thinned out a bit, then take one of the seats that opened up. Only the crowd didn't thin out; more and more people continued to board until the aisle was filled back to front. Sal spent the remainder of the trip wedged in the middle of a line of commuters, everyone pressed together like sardines in a tin.

They rode that way for nearly an hour, the familiar sights of Ashburg passing by on the periphery, until eventually the clusters of houses and shops grew more sporadic, then disappeared altogether. Now they found themselves surrounded by greenery, large grassy expanses interspersed with clusters of fir and pine trees. There was an artificial feel to the landscape, Sal noted, the grass too manicured, the trees too neatly arranged.

The bus slowed and pulled off the main road onto a narrow, winding drive that snaked its way through a stand of evergreens, then up a slope that soon crested and fell away into a shallow valley that had previously been hidden from view. Here, arranged in a grid like a miniature city unto itself, was an industrial park – row after row of blockish, concrete-and-glass structures nearly indistinguishable from one another save for the large numbered signs out front.

The bus threaded its way deeper into the park, until suddenly there was a '*bang!*', and the floor seemed to disappear beneath Sal's feet. Shouts went up all around. Somewhere up ahead a woman shrieked. Now the bus began to vibrate like an unbalanced washing machine, sending its occupants careening into each other like the contents of a martini shaker. Sal had to clutch at the nearest handrail to keep himself from falling, just as he had continued to do every weekday morning since then, right up until the present day.

"Did you hear what I said?" the woman bellowed.

"I heard," said Sal.

"Look at me when I'm talking to you!"

"I can't." Sal gave it another go and found the physics of the situation unchanged. "But if I could, you better believe I would!"

"Why would I believe anything a…a *ragamuffin* like you has to say?"

"Ragamuffin?"

"Don't make me repeat it!"

"Lady, can't you see I'm struggling here?" As if on cue the bus dipped into a pothole, sending Sal stumbling forward, thrusting his pelvis toward the woman's face. "Don't you know how hard it is out there for the little guy? Haven't you read the papers?"

"What are you talking about, papers? Are you on drugs?"

"Take your pick – *The Bugle, The Statesman…*"

"Drugs, all right. I had a nephew like you…"

"…*The New Observer, The Frontiersman…*"

"Airplane glue, that's how it started. Sniff a whole tube then take off running, out of the house and all the way to the zoo…"

"…*The Diplomat, The Gazette, The Intelligencer…*even *The Wall Street Journal…*"

"One time we found him in the Birds of Africa enclosure, eyes rattling around like bingo balls, trying to gnaw the foot off an ostrich."

"All they talk about is the economy, the recession. It's tough out there for a guy like me."

"Ah, a welfare sponge! I should have guessed. Loitering on the bus, rubbing your…*genitalia* on any woman unlucky enough to sit within prodding distance. Trying to get a little something for nothing."

"No ma'am," said Sal. Suddenly his voice grew steely. It was the voice of a marine captain reflecting upon honor, duty, and love of country. Even the old woman was impressed into silence. "No ma'am, as a matter of fact I am at this moment on my way to my place of employ to eke out an honest living through such talents as God has blessed me with, and where such talents fail me through grit and determination. Boastfulness finds no natural home within my person, yet I can state without compunction that I have worked for everything I have in this life and should sooner feel the pangs of hunger than accept a crumb above my earnings."

There was a pause during which – unbeknownst to Sal – the woman regarded him, wondering if she were being conned…with good reason, as Sal had cribbed his speech from an old Reverend Edward Greenfield pamphlet his father had left lying around the house when he was a boy.

"Well," she said, after a moment, "just keep your willy out of my face."

Before he could respond, the door of the bus squealed open. The line of people standing in the aisle began trudging toward the front, pulling Sal along like a twig caught in a river current. He tumbled down the stairs and was deposited on the sidewalk amongst a sea of Dockers khakis and Ann Taylor dresses, the occupants of which blinked their eyes and looked about uncomprehendingly, like shipwrecked sailors who had washed up on a foreign shore.

Sal blinked too, the sun having risen considerably during his time in the bus's gloomy interior. As his eyes adjusted, the first thing he took in was the large aluminum sign reading '17 Industry Way' that fronted the office complex where True North had their sales and processing centers.

"Sal-va-tore!" said a sing-song-y voice from somewhere within the throng. Only one person used Sal's full name, and it was not someone he wished to see so early on a Monday morning. Fumbling for his keycard, he scampered up the steps and across the plaza toward Building C, where he badged himself in through the door to the side stairwell.

He had been using this stairwell to enter and exit the building since the very beginning, rarely if ever passing through the cavernous main lobby with its marble floors that made every footstep echo like a snare drum, and the security guards who made indifferent small talk as they checked everyone's IDs. In contrast to the lobby's modern finishes and clean lines the stairwell seemed to belong to a different building altogether, all concrete and galvanized steel painted a uniform, drab beige that turned the light from the fluorescent lamps overhead a sickly, twilight hue. For Sal it was a respite, a place apart where he could catch his breath and be alone with his thoughts, if only for a few moments.

True North had its offices on the third floor. Sal lunged up the stairs, away from the source of the sing-song-y voice, though he knew there was as little chance of her using the stairwell herself as there was of him avoiding her for long once he finally made it to the office. By the time he reached the landing for the second floor he had begun to slow, and by the time he reached the third floor he was wheezing. Sal wasn't old, exactly, but age for him had ceased to be only a number and brought with it now a series of ever-escalating indignities and barriers that he could do nothing but learn to shoulder. He paused for a moment until he had regained his composure, then swiped his badge again and stepped through the door into True North's gray, carpeted hallways.

A pony-tailed woman appeared out of the gloom. Sal moved aside to let her pass, then headed toward the sales floor. Along the way he glanced through the windows of the customer service and human resources departments. Most of the desks inside were unoccupied. The clocks read fifteen minutes to eight, that strange, transitory time where the office seemed to exist somewhere between dreams and reality. Lights flickered on one by one across the floor, as if a slumbering beast were being roused to consciousness. Those early arrivals who were already seated in their cubicles stopped looking at their phones or aimlessly browsing the internet and began steeling themselves for the day ahead. Every few minutes an elevator by the reception area opened and deposited more bleary-eyed workers into the mix. They shuffled through the halls, subdued and disoriented, like bees through a hive that had just been doused with smoke.

Sal turned left at the end of the hall and started down the adjoining corridor. In the distance, a sign reading 'Sales Dept.' jutted out from the wall, beckoning to him like a military standard. As he drew nearer he began taking out his ID for the third time (*What is all this security for?* he wondered), when a figure materialized in front of him, grinning with piano-key teeth.

"Sal-va-TOR-ay!!!" it sang.

"Hey, Sheila," said Sal.

"I saw you out front and tried getting your attention," she said, "but you must not have heard me."

"Guess not."

Sheila grinned in rebuke (Sal marveled at how Sheila could make a smile mean just about anything) and peered down at the clipboard she was clutching. Sal hadn't noticed it until that moment, but he had known it was there somewhere, the way one observing a dog as it pokes its head into the room knows that its tail will eventually follow. "Now let's see…ee…EE…ee…EE…" she sang.

Sal managed to wrestle his ID from his lanyard and turn toward the door. It was imperative to keep his eyes averted, he knew, as Sheila's grin also possessed an uncanny ability to interrupt and wrest control of a conversation. "Sorry to be pushy, Sheila, but I was late one day last week and Mr. Leathers sent out that communication about punctuality and I just want to make sure I clock in on time, and…"

"No worries!" she said. "I'll follow you to your desk."

"Great."

Sal opened the door and held it for Sheila, who trailed after him like a duckling after its mother. As he wound his way through the maze of cubicles, he offered half-hearted good mornings to the other sales reps who had arrived ahead of him.

"Hey, Doug," said Sal, to a young man ten years his junior who was hunched over his desk, head in hands. "Rough morning?"

"Dude." Doug turned his sunken eyes toward them. His cheeks were dotted with stubble and seemed to glisten, as if he were secreting cooking oil. "You have no idea what I got up to this weekend. It was deranged. Like, no exaggeration. Seriously, Sally, I don't even want to talk about it, that's how…I mean…dude, if you had gotten into *half* of the stuff I got into you wouldn't even be here today, you'd probably need an entire week's vacation just to think about whether you ever wanted to get out of bed again. *Epic* is not the word for it. Even thinking about it makes me nauseous. It's like…"

"Doug Sheets…" said Sheila, looking down at her clipboard.

"Oh, shit," said Doug. "Didn't see you there, Sheila."

"No worries!" Sheila grinned and ran her finger down the page, then gave a satisfied nod. "I see you haven't signed up yet for this weekend's 5k Fun Run to raise money for thrush awareness."

"The bird?" said Doug.

"The fungal infection." Sheila shook her head at Sal. "It just goes to show why this is such an important cause."

"I can't run," said Doug. "After the weekend I had, I can barely see straight. I mean, I've gone *hard* before, but like this…this was like…"

"No, no," said Sheila, "we're looking for sponsors."

"Like…money?"

"Per kilometer or flat rate."

"I pay you to run?"

"You can certainly sponsor *me*, if you want." She fluffed her hair. "I will be running this year, of course. Got my new joggers all broken in."

"How much?"

"How much are they broken in?"

"How much money do you want?"

"Well, I can't tell you how much you should donate, of course…"

"Here." Doug rummaged through his pants pocket and pulled out a wrinkled, wilted bill. He held it out to her. "Is this enough?"

"Five dollars?" Sheila's grin wavered, but managed to hold in the end. She took out a pen and started writing on the clipboard. "That's flat rate, then?"

"The other one," said Doug.

"Hmm." She scratched out what she'd written. "One…dollar…per…kilometer." She plucked the five-dollar bill from Doug's hand as if it were a decaying bird carcass. "And how about you, Sal? Can I put you down for an amount?"

"I don't know." Sal looked around at all the places Sheila wasn't, but couldn't figure out how to get to any of them without her being there when he arrived. "Can I get back to you? I really need to get to my desk and clock in."

"Well get a move on, eager beaver! I'm right behind you." Sheila grinned in a way that told Sal she would follow him to the ends of the Earth, if need be.

Sal said goodbye to Doug and shuffled off toward his cubicle, Sheila hovering behind him like a wolf stalking an injured deer. When he arrived, he collapsed into his swivel chair and turned on his computer, staring blankly at the monitor as it booted up.

"While we're waiting," said Sheila. "I was hoping I could put you down for a fifty-dollar pledge."

"Fifty?!"

"That *is* the average donation nationally, according to the American Society for Thrush Prevention." She batted her eyes, her lashes stirring the air around them like a pair of Japanese fans. "Of course, I know you – like me – believe that we here at the True North family are exceptional, not just average, so if you wanted to give something more than fifty to reflect that…"

"I think…um…" Sal paused, as if meaning to continue his thought, but the pause stretched on and on until at last Sheila lowered her clipboard and leaned in close to examine his face. "Are you feeling ok?" she said.

"What?"

"Your eyes. They look sort of sunken."

"I haven't been sleeping well." He waved his hand, as if it were of no concern.

"You know what I do when I can't sleep?" Sheila took Sal's silence as an invitation to continue. "I close my eyes, lay back on my pillow, and think about all the things I'm thankful for."

"Does it work?"

"Oh, yes." Sheila nodded. "One minute I'm counting my blessings, and the next thing I know the sun is shining through the curtains and it's morning." She took a deep breath and exhaled, as if she had just at that moment awoken from a satisfying night's sleep.

A voice from the other side of the cubicle wall piped up. "Would you rather sleep deeply for eight hours every night and wake up feeling rested, but have terrible nightmares that you remember every detail of, or sleep only four hours a night and feel groggy all the time, but have the most beautiful, exquisite dreams?" A moment later, an angular, bespectacled face leaned out into the aisle and regarded them. "Hello, Sheila," it said.

Sheila's grin collapsed. "Hello, Colleen," she mumbled. "I notice here that *you* aren't listed as a sponsor." She tapped the clipboard. "Should I even bother asking if you'd be interested in participating this year?"

"Nah," said Colleen. "Actually, wait...I'll consider it, *if* you answer my question."

"What question?"

"About the dreams. Good sleep and bad dreams, or bad sleep and good dreams?"

Sheila sighed. It was a sigh only a particular type of southern woman could make, and as an alumnus and former chapter president of Alpha Delta Phi, Sheila was most certainly that type. It conveyed both patience and impatience, selflessness and self-pity, sympathy and disgust, as if paradox were embodied in a single exhalation. "Bless your heart," she said. "I do not answer hypothetical questions."

"Why not?" said Colleen.

"Because if God wanted things a certain way, they would be that way. Hypotheticals are how the Devil tried to confuse Jesus."

"Suit yourself. How about you, Sal?"

"What?"

"The dreams."

"Oh." Sal blinked, feeling the raw redness of his eyes. "I'll take the four hours and good dreams. I can't sleep anyway, so may as well enjoy the time that I do."

Colleen gave a satisfied nod, then looked at Sheila. "See, how hard was that?"

"I cannot deal with this right now." All at once Sheila's demeanor changed. She closed her eyes and stretched out a hand, as if trying to ward off tears. "You try to stay upbeat and do what's right, but it can be so hard sometimes. There has been so much negativity surrounding me lately. Last week, a man threatened to *kill* me!"

"What?" said Sal. "Are you ok?"

"I'm holding together, yes," she said. "It was scary, but my belief in myself has been seeing me through."

"Where did this happen?"

"Over the phone. It was one of the customers. He said he wanted to return his True North system, so I asked him why. He said his compass always pointed at him, no matter how he held it or where he stood. I said congratulations, that means you've achieved enlightenment. He said he was about as enlightened as a dime-store table lamp, and that I must not be any brighter if I believed a load of horseshit like that." She threw up her hands. "Who uses language like that with a woman over the telephone?"

"How did he threaten you?" said Sal.

"He told me he hoped I'd get hit by a bus. A bus!"

"Was that all he said?"

"That's not enough for you? Should he throw in a train for good measure? How about the entire mass transit system?"

"It's not exactly a threat, is all I'm saying."

"It may as well be! If enough people think on something, or even if just one person thinks on it really, really hard, it will manifest itself. I've been witness to this. My best friend, Marlene, found her husband that way." Sheila took a measured breath. "Now I can barely go outside without looking over my shoulder."

"Do you think a bus is following you?" said Colleen.

Sheila gave her a withering look. "There are roads *everywhere*."

"Why didn't you just give him a refund?"

"Hello? A little thing called company policy? Refunds are only honored in cases where the customer demonstrates by clear and convincing evidence that the product was defective."

"Sounds defective to me," said Sal. "If the compass keeps pointing at him."

"It's *supposed* to point at him. That means it's working!"

"The guy said he hoped you'd get hit by a bus," said Sal. "Does that sound enlightened to you?"

"It *sounds* like my coworkers would rather take the easy way out, even if it means playing fast and loose with the company's money."

"Look, Sheila…"

"Fifty dollars?" said Sheila.

"I…um…" Sal shrugged. "Twenty?"

"*Thank* you!" Sheila jotted down the amount on her notepad, then thrust it toward Sal. "Just sign right here," she pointed.

Sal scribbled something meant to be a signature. Sheila took back the clipboard and darted off after a member of the admin staff who had the bad fortune to be passing through her line of sight at exactly that moment.

"She should be over here in sales instead of customer service," said Sal.

"I hate her," said Colleen.

"Come on. She's pushy, but she isn't that bad."

"I saw a true crime show on TV about a woman who looked just like Sheila. She killed her own children with a harpoon."

"That sounds made up."

"That's *exactly* what the woman told police everyone would think!" Colleen narrowed her eyes at Sheila's retreating back, as if even at that moment the latter might be planning some devious crime. "They still caught her, though. Because of the bloody harpoon in her trunk."

"How do you fall asleep, Colleen?" said Sal.

"All alone, in my king-size bed."

"But I mean, do you do anything to help yourself fall asleep?"

"Like pleasuring myself?"

"Jesus!" Sal felt his cheeks go red.

"It's widely accepted that sexual release before bed improves the quality of one's sleep."

"I meant like melatonin or a noise machine…"

"Nope," said Colleen, "just stretch out on my big, empty bed, close my eyes and zonk out."

"Every night?"

She shrugged. "Usually. I get restless sometimes, just like everyone else. When that happens, I have a body pillow I like to use."

"Does it work?"

"Like a charm. I lay it in the bed next to me and cuddle up close…"

"Um…."

"…then I stretch my leg up over it like this…"

"I got it."

"…then slide my other leg under the bottom, wrap them around and just *squeeze*…"

"I got it, Colleen!"

"Hey Sal?"

"Yeah?"

"You'd better punch in, it's five after eight."

Sal looked at the clock and made a choking sound, then dove into his cubicle and jabbed at his computer's power button. After a moment the startup screen appeared, the little circle in the center of the monitor spinning and spinning and spinning. Sal drummed his fingers on his desk, watching the seconds tick by. Eventually the prompt appeared telling him to insert his ID card. He did so, then waited again for the second prompt instructing him to enter his password. This he did – the first time incorrectly, the second time remembering to turn his caps lock off – after which he was rewarded with another spinning circle.

When at last his computer's desktop appeared, he moved the cursor over the timeclock icon and jabbed furiously at his mouse, only to find that the cursor was also spinning and would not respond. Sal watched helplessly as application after application started up, each taking its turn with no apparent haste, like kids in a talent show waiting for the current act to finish before shuffling onstage to begin their own.

When the spinning circle finally morphed into the familiar white arrow, Sal opened the timeclock and clicked on the 'Time In' button. His electronic timecard populated with '8:08 am'. Sal took a deep breath and exhaled. *Only eight minutes*, he thought. *It's not so bad.*

I'll make it up at the end of the day. I bet no one will even notice.

This thought stayed with Sal for the next twelve seconds, exactly the amount of time it took for him to open his email and see the unread message from that morning sitting at the top of his inbox. It was from his boss, Mr. Leathers, and contained no content, only a subject line: "Come to my office immediately!"

Two

If anyone had ever wondered aloud, or even just in one's head, what True North was or where it came from it was almost certainly because of the company's commercials. Turn on the TV during the wee hours of the morning and channel surf through the dregs of basic cable, and in between questionable preachers peddling End-Times prophecy, professional bass fishing tournaments, and reruns of *Cops* you'll almost certainly come across an out-of-focus missive (as if it were filmed using a camcorder thirty years ago) that opens on a man wandering through the desert.

At least, one presumes he's been wandering. Nothing can be seen for miles around but rocky red mesas and a sandy valley floor dotted with cacti. Yet the man is dressed as if for a business lunch. Though he moves with the stilted gait of one who is on the verge of collapse not a drop of sweat can be found on his person, giving him the appearance of someone at a professional conference who has just staggered out of his hotel room after a hard night of partying.

"What does it all mean?" intones a voice in the strident baritone of a right-wing talk radio host; simultaneously, the words appear on the screen in sickly, yellow-ochre lettering. Before we realize it, the backdrop has changed – gone are the man and desert, replaced by a black-and-white image of the Egyptian pyramids, followed closely by time-lapse video of drifting clouds and a stopwatch ticking away the seconds.

"I felt alone," says a man, sitting in what appears to be the kitchen-furnishings section of a Home Depot. "It was like my life was moving in a different direction than everyone else's. I needed help."

"Feeling confused?" says the baritone voice. This time only the word *'confused?'* appears on the screen, complete with question mark. Now another man is standing before us, tall and lanky with a shock of wavy hair standing on end, like a root vegetable that has gained consciousness and wishes to share its thoughts with the human race. "I used to be like you," he says. "Adrift. Passive. Letting life happen to me instead of *creating* the life I deserve."

Now the camera zooms in. We see the man from the waist up. He is looking directly at us. We notice he has a thin mustache, the same sandy-blond color as his hair. "The answers are out there," he insists, as the word *'Answers'* hovers tantalizingly over his right shoulder. We trust this man. He wears a maroon turtleneck under a tan, corduroy jacket.

"Life can be overwhelming," the man says, only in voiceover now. We see a different middle-aged man sitting on a rumpled loveseat in his living room, hunched forward and propping his head up like a more befuddled-looking first draft of Rodin's *The Thinker*.

"You aren't lazy. You're willing to do the work. You just don't know where to begin." The man's gaze turns toward a pair of French doors in the background, as if perhaps the answer lay somewhere on his patio. "What you need is someone to point you in the right direction. Someone to show you your *true north*."

Now a different man is there, wearing a fitted, V-neck t-shirt and giving off the vague impression that he has just worked out. Some text in the bottom-left corner of the screen informs us that this is 'Jalen B.', and that he is a True North customer. "I wanted to change, but I didn't know how," he says into the camera, waving his hands about as if concerned you might not be paying attention. "True North gave me the wisdom to chart my own course and the confidence to follow it to the end."

"The journey can be difficult," says Sandra S., an energetic young woman who nods her head as she speaks, as if realizing for the first time that she agrees with everything she's saying. "But nothing valuable is easy, and I can't think of anything that's proven more valuable in allowing me to live my best life than True North."

True North

"True North draws from the four Cardinal and four Ordinal wisdoms," says the voice of the man in the corduroy jacket. A series of still images cycles past, including a statue of the Buddha with the sun rising behind it, a drawing of Rene Descartes pointing at a map, and a group of Orthodox rabbis shouting at one another across a picnic table. "The same principles that have guided many of history's great thinkers and form the backbone of the world's major religions."

Now we see the man again as he walks, slowly but purposefully, across a room, the camera panning right to left to follow him. In his hand is a compass. "I will give you the tools to unlock the secrets to success, happiness, and peace of mind. The answers are there, inside of you. Let True North help you discover them." As he says this, the man waves the compass in the air, then holds it out in front of him. "The path to a new life starts with a single step." Now the camera jumps to show the compass's face. The needle is pointing straight back, directly at the man's chest. "Make sure it's the right step. Call now."

The baritone voice returns to inform us that we can order our True North motivational system for only $49.99, plus processing and handling. Along the bottom of the screen, a phone number and website where you can place your order flash with the urgency of a hurricane warning. In the center of the screen we see the True North system itself, a cardboard box with the lid removed and its contents spread out on the table in front of it, including an audio CD, a workbook, the True North instructional manual, a deck of 'daily affirmation' cards, and most prominently a compass like the one the man in the corduroy jacket was holding.

The compass is not a gimmick. That is to say, it is not a toy; it is a real, working compass, albeit of dubious quality. True North's claim that those who follow its program will know that they've achieved enlightenment when the compass points directly at them *may* be a gimmick. That was for the FTC to decide, argued the company's execs.

What was definitively not a gimmick was when the compass pointed at the man in the commercial, the founder and CEO of True North, LLC, Burt Leathers. *All* compasses pointed toward Leathers whenever he came close enough, no television magic required. They had been doing so ever since that fateful day when he himself had achieved enlightenment. He was a walking testament to the company's veracity, a one-man bulwark against charges of fraud.

At least, that's how he felt about it. Proving he had "achieved enlightenment and gained access to the wisdom of the Ages" may prove exceedingly difficult in a civil suit, True North's chief counsel had warned him. To Leathers, however, it was self-evident. He was wealthy, successful, and totally at ease with himself and his place in the universe. And it all stemmed from his moment of revelation, that glorious day thirty years earlier when the truth had been revealed to him in a blinding flash of light.

To be fair, Leathers would concede if pressed, he couldn't say precisely what he had done to bring about this revelation, nor could he remember much of the moment itself. It existed on the fringes of his memory, a ghostly impression like the remains of a dream from one's childhood.

Or, in the case of Leathers, childhood itself. One thing he had never admitted to anyone was that since achieving enlightenment he could no longer remember anything of his life before that moment. This was disconcerting for a man who prided himself on his wisdom and certainty about the world. In his daily life he was no different than anyone else. He remembered names and faces; knew his own name, address, and phone number; went to work, came home, went shopping, ran errands, etc. There was a continuity from day to day that formed what most people think of as an identity, a life. But try to work backwards through his memory and he would inevitably come up against that moment, the continuity crashing against it and dissipating like a wave hitting a breakwater. He *knew* that he had had a childhood, that he had had parents and a family, had gone to school, had grown up. Yet none of it was there, inside his head. Just the last thirty years and a flash of light that had started it all.

This was difficult for Leathers to reconcile. *A man without a past has no future*, went a famous quote, and while Leathers felt compelled to argue the truth of it – to point out the incredible success he had achieved with little past to speak of – he could not pretend that he didn't feel adrift at times. The harder he tried to remember what had come before the more his memory resisted, and the deeper he felt its absence. A general uneasiness haunted him, a sense that he was living a lie and would be made to suffer the consequences. Sometimes it pushed its way to the fore, and he would banish it with great effort and concentration. But it never left him completely, just retreated to the back of his mind, a low, dull hum biding its time until he grew slack and let his guard down again. Time and quietude were his enemies, and so Leathers remained busy, focusing on the things he could control – namely the daily operations of True North.

He was in his office, in the middle of checking his email, when there was a knock at the door. "Yes?" he said. The door inched open (*tentatively*, noted Leathers; he was a firm believer that one could learn a lot about a person by how he or she opened a door), and a head poked itself around the corner. "You wanted to see me?" it said.

"Come in," said Leathers, gesturing toward the young man, who slid sideways into the room without opening the door any further, as if he were scuttling between two closely parked cars. *Yes,* thought Leathers, *very tentative.* Well, he wasn't surprised. An email saying to see the boss first thing in the morning could be unnerving for anyone. Leathers gestured to the chairs on the other side of his desk. "Have a seat, Salvatore," he said.

Sal nodded and reached for a chair, then hesitated. His hand gripped the backrest of the chair on his right. He began to pull it out, but stopped and turned toward the lefthand chair, giving it and the desk a quick scan before settling on the righthand one. He finished pulling it out and lowered himself, gradually, onto the seat, as if reserving the right to change his mind until the very last moment.

"Not everything is a test," said Leathers.

"I know," said Sal. "*Sir*...I know, sir. I was just making sure I chose the best seat."

"And what makes the best seat?"

Sal scrunched up his face. Leathers studied him, weighing the man, letting his intuition – his *compass*, as he would put it – guide him. He found it particularly difficult in this case. Normally he could get a read on someone within minutes of meeting them, but there was something familiar about this young man that distracted him. It was the same familiarity that had made Leathers interested in him in the first place. Given his dearth of memories it was a sensation Leathers was unused to, and wondering over it had begun taking up more and more of his mental energy over the course of the last year.

"Lots of things, I suppose," said Sal, after some thought. "The height, the width…how comfortable the cushions are, the way the seat slants…how it's situated in the room…"

"Is that why you were late this morning?" said Leathers. "Trying to make sure every last detail was perfect?"

"That wasn't my fault!" said Sal. "Sheila was asking for donations for the thrush walk. Every time I tried to get away, she kept on…"

Leathers held up a hand to stop him. "Listen, son…may I call you son?"

"I'd rather you didn't."

"Well, I'm going to do it anyway. Not to be condescending or as some big-prick show of authority, but because I feel compelled to. I've gotten to where I am today by following my instincts. My True North, you might say." He flashed a grin, which Sal returned half-heartedly. "Not by blaming others for my mistakes. Do you understand where I'm coming from?"

"Sorry, sir. I didn't mean to blame, just wanted to explain what happened."

"You ever heard the saying, *An explanation is just an excuse that got too big for its britches*?"

"I don't think so, sir."

"I just came up with it. What do you think?"

"I'm not sure I understand."

"That's ok. Feel free to use it, see if it catches on. Did you know that every famous phrase started out just like this, one person talking to another?"

"I suppose I did. I guess I never really thought about it before." Sal fidgeted through the intervening silence. When it became clear that Leathers was not going to speak further, he swallowed through a clenched throat and said, "Am I in trouble, sir?"

Leathers hand fell on the desk with a mighty *'bang!'*, so jarring that Sal nearly leapt from his chair. "Now we're getting somewhere," said Leathers. "Rip off the Band-Aid! A real leader must never be afraid to acknowledge and confront the truth head on."

Sal frowned. "So…I am in trouble?"

"That depends." Leathers pushed out his chair, stood, and placed his hands behind his back in the attitude of a boarding-school headmaster. He began to pace. As his office was little bigger than a walk-in closet, however, he quickly ran out of room, and instead took to pivoting from side to side like one of those wind-up mouse toys for cats. "Do you consider hard work to be trouble? Do long hours and greater responsibility sound like a punishment to you?"

Yes, thought Sal, though he knew enough not to say so out loud. "I don't understand," he said.

"I'm getting old." Leathers studied his coatrack, as if measuring the bygone years by the garments which had once hung there. He sighed. "No, it's no use. I know what you're going to say – *you've got plenty of good years left in you*. I don't deny it. I'm not here fishing for compliments. But when a man reaches my age he starts to look at his legacy, the things he'll leave behind. He wants to make sure those things will be well taken care of when he's gone."

"You're dying?" said Sal.

"We're all dying," said Leathers. "The important thing is to optimize the time that we're alive." He shot Sal a meaningful look. "Chapter One, Part Three of the True North instructional manual. This isn't just a way for me to make money. It's the moral framework I use to structure my life."

Sal nodded. Talk like this made him uncomfortable. He had heard Leathers express similar sentiments at all-hands meetings and to the press, and of course on the company's television ads. He had always taken it for granted that it was salesman's patter, and perhaps it was. Certainly, that was how Sal meant it when he said similar things to the customers who called in with questions about whether or not True North really worked. Maybe Leathers never stopped selling, even when he was alone. Was that all the best salespeople were, Sal wondered, method actors who so intensely embodied their roles that they ended up deceiving themselves in order to better deceive the public?

For True North was a deception, of that Sal was sure, just the latest iteration in a long line of positive-thinking, quick-fix mumbo jumbo. The fact that Leathers seemed to genuinely believe in it unnerved Sal. Whether that was because of what it said about the older man's judgment, or what Sal's own lack of belief said about his character, he wasn't sure. After all, they both made a living telling people the same things. Which was worse, to be a zealot or a hypocrite?

"Are you paying attention?" said Leathers.

Sal snapped back to the present. While he had been musing, Leathers had come around to perch on the edge of his desk, just inches from where Sal sat. The older man loomed over him like an oak tree towering over a toadstool.

"Yes, sorry," said Sal. "Sometimes I like to take what people are telling me and really sit with it for a moment, chew it over, you know? It can come across like I'm not interested, but in fact, I'm *extra* interested, so to speak. That is, if you will. There's a Chinese proverb that says a single day whispers infinite truths, if only we are wise enough to hear them. I've always said that listening is easy, but *hearing* is an art form." He cleared his throat. "Again, if you will."

"Seems like you have quite a few sayings."

"The many fruits of my listening." He held up a finger. "That is, hearing."

Leathers nodded. "A deep thinker. Humble, not afraid to learn. I respect that. That's exactly the type of person True North needs at the helm, steering it into the future."

True to what he had just said, it took Sal several seconds to process the words that Leathers had spoken. Even after he had mulled them over and eliminated every possible alternative explanation, he couldn't accept that they meant what he ultimately concluded they must. "You want me to take over the company?" he said, at last.

"Son, what did you think this was all about? Punching in late?" Leathers waved a hand. "Plebian concerns. The leaders, the visionaries...we have more important things to worry about than arbitrary rules. Genius doesn't run on a schedule."

"It doesn't?"

Leathers shook his head. A peculiar sensation formed in Sal's stomach, then quickly spread throughout his body to the furthest extremities. His skin tingled; for a moment he worried his childhood eczema might be coming back. He felt sweaty yet was covered in goosebumps, as if he were running a fever. "Mr. Leathers, I'm beginning to suspect that you may be making fun of me."

True North

"Fun?" said Leathers. "Son, there's nothing fun about contemplating your own mortality, believe me. But it's something we all have to face eventually, from the exalted to the mean. The great evener, death. We're all the same height lying down."

"Are you saying", said Sal, "that everyone is as tall lying down as they are standing up? Or that everyone becomes the same height as each other when they lie down?"

"The second one," said Leathers. "Not head-to-toe, of course. More like if you start at the ground and measure upwards."

"Either way I don't think that's true."

"It's figurative." Leathers frowned. Sal suspected it had been another one of his own sayings.

"Why me, though, sir?" said Sal. "I don't believe we've ever spoken before today."

"Son, there are two maxims I've always followed when I need to make a big decision – 'be prepared…do your homework'…"

"Those sort of sound like the same thing."

"That's just the first one. I was saying it two different ways. It's 'be prepared' and 'follow your gut'. Those might sound contradictory, but they're equally important. You can't make a sound decision without having all the necessary information. I know that to all of you out on the floor I might seem distant sometimes, shut away in my office. But I assure you I'm paying

35

attention to everything that's going on out there. Nothing happens in this workplace that I don't know about. I won't go into exactly how I know, but rest assured I have my ways."

Leathers gave Sal a meaningful look, only continuing after the latter nodded in acknowledgment. "Even so, all the information in the world can't tell you with one-hundred percent accuracy which decision is the right one. That's where the gut comes in. Sometimes you just get a feeling. And I've got a feeling about you."

A side effect of sleep deprivation is the muting of emotions. Perhaps that accounted for the blank look on Sal's face that greeted his boss's assessment. Whatever the cause, it was not the reaction Leathers had anticipated. *This might be more complicated than I expected,* he thought to himself.

"How does that make you feel?" he said, as Sal continued to gape like a trout in a fishmonger's window.

"Gee, I don't know," said Sal. He had never been asked such a question before. No one had ever taken an interest in his feelings.

"Let me ask you this," said Leathers. "Are you proud of the work you do here?"

"Yes," Sal answered automatically, and was surprised to find that he meant it. Logically he knew there was nothing to be proud of, convincing people to hand over their hard-earned money in exchange for a bunch of platitudes bundled together and wrapped up in pretty packaging. Nevertheless, the fact that he was so good at it *was* a source of pride for him. He had never excelled at something before. It felt good to be able to live up to someone else's expectations, to be accepted as part of a team. For the first time in his life, he felt like he belonged somewhere.

Leathers nodded. "And do you think you're up to the job?"

"I couldn't honestly say, sir. I'm not sure what the job entails."

"Don't fixate on the details." Leathers leaned forward until his face was level with Sal's, peering into the latter's eyes as if screening for cataracts. He pointed to his gut. "I'm asking you to look in here. Are you ready to take on this challenge?"

Sal shifted in his seat. He felt a strange sensation in the pit of his stomach, one that quickly spread outward and crept up into his chest. It was not the butterflies he had felt when he first entered Leathers' office. Anxiety was a feeling he knew well, one which had only gotten worse as his sleep deteriorated. This was something else altogether, a vibration, as if someone were thrumming his nerves like guitar strings. It continued to spread, coursing through the whole of his body. His skin prickled, the hairs on his arms and legs stood on end. He curled and uncurled his toes reflexively, and wrung his hands. It wasn't painful, exactly, but deeply uncomfortable, as if his blood vessels were electrical wires through which an increasingly strong current was being pumped.

Leathers hovered in front of Sal, waiting for a response. "Yes," said Sal at last. He wasn't even sure anymore what the question had been, only that he needed to get away as soon as possible. It was becoming increasingly hard to keep it together. His teeth felt as though they were trying to loosen themselves from his gums, and it took all of his willpower to make his clenched jaw form words. "Absolutely," he managed, adding a short nod.

"Good." Leathers patted Sal on the shoulder, then stood and went around to the other side of his desk. Almost immediately the sensation dissipated. Sal blinked at the sudden relief and looked around, disoriented, like someone who'd just woken up in an unfamiliar room.

"Let's meet later today to start your orientation," said Leathers. "I'll have Sunset email you an invite with the details. I'm also going to have her work on some messaging to the floor."

He leaned over a stack of papers on his desk and began leafing through them, but raised his head again as Sal started to get up. "Obviously, I'd prefer if you don't tell anyone about this until the announcement comes out. We should have all the paperwork drafted and ready for you to sign by tomorrow, Wednesday at the latest. I'll get Legal on it."

"Wait a minute," said Sal. "You're letting me take over right now? I thought this was about planning for the future."

"Tomorrow's the future, isn't it?" Leathers grinned. "Besides, all I said was that this is about making sure my company is taken care of when I'm gone. I never said when I'd be leaving."

"But I don't know what I'm doing!"

"That's what orientation is for." Leathers' smile grew wider. He gestured breezily, like someone who had just been told by the doctor that his tumor was benign. "Like I said, you'll get an invite." He waved a hand in the general direction of the door and went back to sifting through his documents. It took Sal a moment to realize that the conversation was over and he had been dismissed.

The salesfloor looked very different to Sal as he returned from Leathers' office. Not that anything had changed – the layout and décor were exactly as they had been throughout the entire time Sal had worked there – but he looked at it now through the eyes of a feudal lord surveying his lands. Unlike a lord, however, he had no ancient bloodline to justify his newfound authority. He walked sheepishly back to his desk, feeling like a fraud, as images of rioting peasants and guillotines flashed through his head.

"You look terrible," said Colleen, peering around the wall of Sal's cubicle as he sat down.

"Thanks," said Sal.

"Really, like garbage," she said. "What happened? Did you get fired? Did Mr. Leathers fire you? Because you're always punching in late? Did you get fired for being late all the time?"

"I don't know what happened." Sal stared at the back of his cubicle like a child who'd been placed in timeout. "Can I ask you a question?" he said, after a moment.

"Sure," said Colleen.

"If someone offered you something really valuable, but you weren't sure you deserved or even wanted it, what would you do?"

"Like monogrammed sheets?"

"Bigger than that. Something that would fundamentally alter your life from that day forward."

"Like a grand piano?"

Sal shook his head. "Bigger. Something that comes with a lot of responsibility, but you aren't sure you've earned the trust that the other person is showing in you by making the offer."

"Ah, like a prize racehorse. I would take it and just ride it around in my backyard. If it gets too expensive you could always sell it, or even just give it away. Did you know there are islands off the coast of Virginia where herds of wild horses live? Maybe you could take it there and set it free."

"Thanks, Colleen."

"Hey, Sal?"

"Yeah?"

"Can I ask you something now?"

"Sure."

"What if your hands were tubes of toothpaste?"

"How do you mean?"

"Let's say instead of a hand you had a tube of toothpaste at the end of each arm."

"Mint or cinnamon flavored?"

"Mint."

"The regular tubes, right? Not the pump things?"

"Oh yes, the regular kind."

"Are the caps on the tubes?"

"Good question!" Colleen's face lit up. One of the reasons she liked Sal so much was because he was the only one in the office who took her questions seriously. "I would think so, yes."

"Then I guess I wouldn't do much of anything," he said at last. "What can anyone do with toothpaste tubes for hands?"

"Exactly!" she said. "People's first impulse is always to say, *well, I guess I'd brush my teeth a lot*, but you wouldn't, would you? How would you hold the brush?" A look of admiration came over her face. "You really are a clever guy, Sal. Everyone thinks so."

"They do?"

"Oh yeah, I can tell. I'm not even sure what you're doing here on the salesfloor with us. I've always thought you seem like the management type."

"Really?"

"Definitely."

"Colleen?"

"Yeah?"

"Thank you."

"For what?"

Sal swiveled in his chair to look at her. "For making my decision for me."

"Decision?" she said, before putting a hand to her mouth. "Oh, the racehorse! Good for you. Just remember to brush it every day. That's as much as I know about horses. The rest you can probably google or get from a book."

"I will." Sal grinned. Colleen blushed and retreated back to her own cubicle.

When he was sure she had gone for good and no one was observing him, Sal sat back in his chair, crossed his left leg over his right knee, and straightened his spine. He kept his shoulders wide, arms relaxed and at his sides, and projected what he hoped was a powerful bearing toward the imaginary audience facing him. There was no mirror handy to confirm for him how he looked, only his monitor, which had turned off from inactivity. In the middle of the screen he could barely make out his shrunken, ghostly reflection surrounded by darkness.

Three

    The cowboy hat was the first thing anyone saw and about the only thing anyone paid attention to. Its brim was as wide as Saturn's rings and cleaved a path around him that gave the impression that here walked a dangerous man, one whom people in crowded places instinctively gave a wide berth. To the contrary, few men in the Alamo Bar & Grill – the establishment into which he had just wandered, looking to grab a bite to eat – posed less of a threat to the general welfare. And while he may not have inspired fear amongst the patrons there, Don Bagley was nevertheless a man they did their best to avoid.

    He'd bought the hat after watching an episode of *Bonanza*, the one where the outlaw, Six Guns Malloy, had ridden his horse onto the Ponderosa beneath a jet-black, ten-gallon Stetson and challenged the whole durned Cartwright clan to a duel. TV had taught him that a good cowboy hat went a long way toward establishing a man's bona fides. It had taught him many other specious lessons as well, including a warped code of honor that demanded revenge for any perceived slight inflicted upon him. It was revenge that propelled him now, two days and more than a thousand miles from home, toward the city of Ashburg and the corporate headquarters of True

North. For Don Bagley had been slighted, and True North – the alleged perpetrator in this instance – had to pay.

He was the sort of man who walked into a bar and said, "I need a drink!" loud enough for everyone to hear. There was a quality of playacting to everything he said or did, as if his life were one long audition for a casting director he thought might be watching from an undisclosed location. "Hoo!" he said, pulling out a stool with his foot and collapsing onto it. "One of them days, huh?" This last question was posed to no one in particular, and as such no one responded. Bagley scooched the stool up toward the bar until he was within elbows' reach, then waved down the bartender and ordered a beer.

"What kind of beer?" said the bartender.

This threw Bagley, as no one on TV ever had to specify the type of beer they wanted; they just said "gimme a beer", and a bottle would appear in front of them a moment later. "Whatever ya got," he said.

The bartender shrugged and rummaged through the cooler, yanking out the first bottle his fingers closed around. "Here you go," he said, setting it on the bar.

"What's Mervin's?" said Bagley, reading the label.

The bartender picked up the bottle again and studied it. "Says here it's the discerning man's lager."

"Yeah?"

The bartender nodded. "Brewed in Almandine, Missouri."

"Well." Bagley looked on mutely as the bartender took his bottle opener and wrenched off the cap. "Bottoms up!"

The bartender made a sour face and drifted off to the other side of the bar. Bagley made his own sour face – the beer tasted peculiar, as if someone had poured it through an old carburetor before serving. "Hey," said Bagley, "they manufacture engine parts in Almandine?"

The bartender was far enough away that he pretended not to hear. Bagley didn't press the issue, but he did ask for a menu. This time the bartender responded, pulling a greasy, laminated sheet from under the sink and handing it to him. Bagley perused the offerings, leaning back on his stool and running his finger along the page as if going over that day's stock ticker in the *Financial Times.*

"Lotta meat on here," he commented.

"It's a menu," said the bartender.

"I'm a real meat man, myself."

"You don't say."

Bagley turned the menu over, then did it again. "I just can't decide." He sighed. "What would you recommend?"

"I don't know," said the bartender.

"You have a favorite thing on this menu?"

"Nope."

"No?"

"That's what I said."

"How can you not have a favorite?"

"I don't like the food here."

"Any of it?"

"Nope."

"There must be something."

"There ain't."

"Even if you don't like the food, you can still have a favorite."

"Oh, Jesus."

"What if you had to eat something? What would you choose?"

"I wouldn't."

"But pretend you had to."

"I don't. There's a sandwich shop right down the street."

"But pretend there wasn't…"

"Why would I do that?"

"Look," said Bagley, "I just want to know what I should eat. I've been on the road all day, and I'm starving."

"Then order anything. What's it matter?"

"I suppose you're right." He sighed again. "Let me have the Rodeo Burger."

47

The bartender snatched the menu and shouted Bagley's order through the door to the kitchen. A flurry of Spanish words drifted back in the opposite direction. The bartender wandered away again, leaving Bagley to nurse his beer. It tasted, he decided, like someone had dropped a handful of iron filings into a regular beer and left them to steep overnight.

"They sure do got funny tastes over in Almandine," he muttered.

"You got that right," said a voice off to Bagley's side. The sound of it sent flutters through his stomach and up and down the length of his spine, which is another way of saying that it belonged to a woman. Bagley looked over and saw a middle-aged female, her dirty-blond hair pulled back in a loose ponytail, staring down into her beer glass. "You get used to it, though," she said. "Spend enough years sucking this stuff down and you even start to miss it a little once you can't find it anymore."

In the intervening seconds before Bagley responded he performed a sort of forensic evaluation. It was an automatic response that occurred whenever he came in contact with a woman, as reflexive as the twitch of his leg whenever the doctor whacked his knee with that little hammer. She was a bit long in the tooth perhaps, but then so was he. The years had been hard, etched into her face in deep grooves, like glacial striations. Still, there was a glint in her eyes that seemed welcoming, a tiny glimmer of girlish mischievousness that hadn't yet been extinguished. Bagley watched as she shifted her weight, uncrossing her legs before crossing them the other way, and twisted on her stool to face him. She had curves in all the right places, as well as some of the wrong ones, which suited him just fine.

"You an Almandine girl?" he said.

The woman laughed, a surprisingly delicate sound, revealing two rows of nicotine-stained teeth that Bagley was happy to see were all present and accounted for. "In a manner of speaking, I suppose," she said. "Not born and raised, mind you, but I spent some good years working out that way at a distribution center."

"Interesting."

She raised her eyebrows. "Is it?"

"Not really." Bagley chuckled and looked down at the floor. "I'm not sure why I said that."

"Because you're trying to flirt with me."

"Oh?" Bagley felt his cheeks grow warm. "Guess I'm doing a pretty rotten job of it."

"Keep going," she grinned. "You're doing fine."

"Now I don't know what to say."

"Maybe you should ask me my name and go from there."

"What's your name, darling?"

"Elmie."

"Elmie? What the hell kind of name is that?"

"It's *my* name, Elmie Duncan."

"Like the donuts?"

"Like Duncan Hines."

"Don't they make donuts?"

"No, they make the cake mix and frosting and whatnot."

"Those are some good donuts."

"They don't make donuts!"

"I mean the other ones."

"I don't go in for any of that stuff." Elmie shook her head. "Sugar's worse for you than cocaine. Any doctor will tell you."

"You never once ate a Dunkin' Donut?"

"Not a one."

Bagley's eyes scanned Elmie top to bottom, a dubious expression on his face. Elmie frowned. "What was that I said about you being just fine at flirting?"

"Aw, horse cocks." Bagley reached up and grasped the brim of his hat, the way he always did when he didn't know what else to do. "I'm sorry. I'm just…I'm dumb as a shovel, Elmie. How about you tell me about yourself and I'll just shut up for a bit? What do you do for a living? Tell me about that distribution center you worked at."

"That oughta heat things up. Ok, fair enough, you asked for it. Well…it was a big old warehouse out in the middle of nowhere – like I said, Almandine – filled to the brim with this wackadoo motivational system you could order by phone. The orders came in, we packaged them up and shipped them off." She took a sip of her Mervin's. "Scintillating, right? I warned you."

"Work is work I suppose," said Bagley. "You ever try it out?"

"Try what out?"

"The motivational system."

"Hell," said Elmie. "I got plenty of motivation. What I need is money. Maybe a handsome millionaire to sweep me off me feet." She ran her finger around the rim of her glass. "You got a spare million or two under that lid of yours?"

"Lid? Oh…" Bagley grabbed onto the brim of his hat again. "Can't say as I do. I have taken a motivational course, though."

"You?"

"You surprised?"

"Kind of. You don't seem like the type."

"I'm not anymore. Thing was a waste of money. Some load of horse crap called True North."

"Get out of town!" Elmie's eyes went wide. She put her purse on the bar and dug around inside, at last removing a plastic card that she slid across to where Bagley was sitting. "Check the bottom-left corner, right below my picture."

"True North, LLC," read Bagley. "I'll be, *that's* who you used to work for?"

"Yep. I'd recognize that box with the stupid compass on the front in my sleep. It's practically all I looked at for the better part of four years."

"And you never gave it a try?"

Elmie arched an eyebrow. "Should I have?"

Bagley smiled. "I s'pose not. Unless you like getting ripped off."

"I don't. That's why I quit. They weren't much better as a boss than they were as a motivator."

"You ever meet the boss?"

"The owner? I don't even know what he looks like."

"You never seen the commercials?"

"I don't watch TV." Elmie took a sip of her beer. "Even if I did, I'd change the channel if I ever saw an ad from those crooks. Worst bunch I ever worked for."

"At least they let you keep this." Bagley waved around the card.

"They didn't *let* me, per se."

"Why you little…" Bagley chuckled. "Thieving is a serious offense, you know."

"I'm not without my naughty side." Elmie slid from her stool and came toward Bagley. When she was next to him, she let her fingertips brush against his knee, then slide up the length of his thigh. "When I get back let's change the subject. Something a little more…pleasurable."

Bagley turned and watched over his shoulder as Elmie wiggled past the bar and through the door to the ladies' room. A burning sensation flared up in his chest, then sank down to his belly where it became a dull ache, as if he'd swallowed a box of jacks. He knew what he was leaving on the table if he slipped out now, but there was nothing for it. Kismet had gifted him an opportunity. He was not such a fool that he would shun it just to know the pleasures of a woman (however rare such pleasures had become).

Bagley had his naughty side, too. Slipping the ID card into his shirt pocket, he tipped his hat to the bartender and made a beeline for the parking lot. Outside, he located his cherry-red Tercel, parked just where he'd left it beside a low wooden fence, looking like a prize courser tethered to its hitching post. He hopped in, fired up the engine, and tore off down the highway into the night.

For his part, the bartender was so happy to see the back of Bagley that he hardly minded the latter had slipped away without paying for his Rodeo Burger. Elmie, however, was not so sanguine. Though Bagley couldn't have known it when he hightailed it for the exit, he was not the first man to disappear from Elmie's life. As she stared down at the now empty barstool where he had been moments earlier, however, she vowed that he would be the last.

Four

"Are you busy?"

Stilton Farnsworth frowned into the receiver, just as he had frowned when his office phone's caller-ID screen had first lit up to reveal his wife's number. He had asked Grace more times than he could remember to refrain from using his work number and instead call him on his personal cell. Propriety was the justification he gave for this request, but in actuality it was because of the greater flexibility it allowed him when trying to avoid her calls.

The life of True North, LLC's chief counsel was a busy one, and a great deal of that business necessitated the turning off of his cell phone, whether for confidentiality reasons or simply to avoid unwanted distractions. His office phone, however, was always available, and if it so happened that his wife called while he was in a meeting, Sunny – that is, Sunset, Mr. Leathers' personal assistant, whose services he had graciously decided to share with the rest of the senior leadership team – would be sure to let him know the moment he was free. As such his requests went unheeded, met by his wife with a brief nod of the head and a promise to comply and then summarily ignored thereafter. When he dared to question why she didn't call his personal phone like he had asked, she would simply say, "I forgot," the excuse as perfunctory as the expressions of concern she made at the beginning of each call.

"I hope I'm not interrupting anything important," she said, not waiting for confirmation before launching into her reason for calling. "I need money."

Stilton Farnsworth's frown deepened. His mouth looked like a croquet wicket. "You have money."

"More of it, I mean."

Stilton said nothing. There was a sigh on the other end of the phone as Grace came to terms with the fact that her demands would need to be accompanied by an explanation. "It's for a *project*," she said.

"What sort of project?"

"Stilty, I've told you before that I can't just sum up my art for you like one of your legal briefs."

Had his mouth not reached its physical limitations Stilton's frown would have deepened even further. His dislike of his given name was exceeded only by that of the many diminutives people used in its place – primarily 'Stilty' where his wife was concerned, and 'Stilt' amongst his coworkers. *What on earth was mother thinking naming me after a cheese?* he wondered, not for the first time. Abandoning the frown, he consoled himself with grinding his teeth. "Is it a painting or sculpture or…?"

"It's everything," she said. "I'm exploring the universality of our biological thought-sphere, provoking instinctive responses that illuminate our collective sense of the sublime."

"So is it a painting or sculpture or…?

Another sigh, this one impatient and tinged with condescension, as if addressed to an insufficiently deferential waiter. "It's an *instructional method*, if you must label it."

"An instructional method?" said Stilton. "You want to take a class?"

"I'm giving the *classes*, as you call them. Helping others to plumb personal experience to craft narratives that aim at a void signifying precisely the non-being of what it represents. From a feminist point of view, of course."

"Why do you need money to teach classes? Shouldn't your students be paying you?"

"Oh, right, like *drawing lessons, twenty dollars an hour* or something?" She scoffed. "I'm not some spinster teaching neighborhood kids piano, Stilty. This is art."

"And the money you want me to give you would be used for…?"

"Studio space, supplies, promotional materials…"

Stilton could envision her counting off each item on her fingers. "Look, now's not a good time, Grace…"

"Graciela," she said.

Stilton narrowly avoided grinding his teeth into powder. "I've told you before, you can call yourself whatever you want professionally, but I am your husband and I'm going to call you by your real name."

"Graciela Sandoval *is* my real name, Stilty."

"Grace Sanders is your name. Your parents are Herb and Ruth Sanders of Waukesha, Wisconsin. Remember them? Graciela Sandoval is something you made up."

"All names are made up."

"I don't have time to get philosophical." Stilton looked forlornly at the half-written brief on his computer. "My appeal is due in three days, and I'm nowhere close to finished. I'm going to need to bring in outside help again, which is going to cost us. It's pretty last-minute, so we'll probably get charged a premium. Not to mention the filing fee and other court costs. So as you can see, we're in a temporary liquidity squeeze, and…"

"Oh *no*," groaned Grace. "Not your stupid case again. Why don't you just let it go, Stilty?"

"How can you say that?"

"You have a good job, with a good salary. If not for this lawsuit we'd have plenty of money."

"Plenty of money? When I win this thing, we'll have enough money for you to put on as many art shows as you want. Hell, I'll buy you your own gallery!"

"That's sweet," said Grace. Stilton could hear her frowning through the phone.

"You don't think I can do it, do you?" he said. "You don't believe in me."

It wasn't that Grace did not believe in Stilton so much as the merits of his case, which – as the First District Court of Appeals had ruled – were non-existent. This was in direct contradiction to what a Boynton County jury had previously found, which was that Stilton Farnsworth had been the victim of an intentional and malicious fraud perpetrated on him by the institution that awarded him his law degree – namely, Harvard Law School.

To Grace, the appeals court panel judges, and most neutral observers this said more about the denizens of Boynton County – their intelligence, their dislike of 'ivory-tower eggheads', or some combination of the two – than anything else. But Stilton took it as a sign that he was on to something, and he refused to give up even after a higher court had laughed him out of the building.

Ironically, Stilton's acumen as a lawyer directly undercut his argument that his education had been insufficient, and that Harvard should reimburse his tuition and compensate him for the three years he "could have been pursuing a more fruitful academic or professional path". His case had been so expertly made, his victory in Boynton County District Court so miraculous, that the First District Court of Appeals found that he had displayed "education and training of the highest order". The Boynton County judgment was vacated in full, without Stilton seeing a penny of his winnings.

He moped for a few days, neglecting Grace and his work at True North to sip Scotch whisky and read through the appeals court's written judgment again and again. It reached the point where Mr. Leathers had to call Stilton into his office for a heart-to-heart. As Stilton slumped glassy-eyed in one of his armchairs, Leathers regaled him with motivational pablum from the True North daily-affirmation card deck. "It's when you're flat on your back that you most clearly see the sky is the limit," he would recite, to give but one example, then turn the card over and place it in one of the many piles or rows he had begun forming on his desk, as if playing some complicated variant of solitaire.

Stilton wasn't sure how many cards Leathers had gone through – at least enough that it necessitated him breaking open the expansion pack that True North had debuted the previous spring – but eventually one of them had broken through his mental haze and set him on his current course. "Every obstacle is an opportunity in disguise," the card had said. Not terribly original, but for Stilton it had opened up a line of attack he had not considered until then – if his win in Boynton County Court had been proof of his skill as an attorney, then wasn't his subsequent loss on appeal a significant counterpoint? How could the First Circuit claim that his was a legal mind of "considerable intelligence and cunning" while simultaneously sneering at his brief as if it had been penned by some serial letter-to-the-editor-writing crank?

The more he thought about it the more he became convinced of the unfairness of it all, the surest antidote to a measured, rational response. He sprang from his chair and bounded from Leathers' office with such enthusiasm that the latter man could hardly take offense at the unceremonious exit, seeing it as further proof of True North's ability to unleash one's animal spirits.

Ever since that moment Stilton had been hard at work on his appellate brief, to the detriment of all else. The time and expense that had gone into his original lawsuit had not been compensated by the ensuing judgment; only another expensive legal proceeding had followed, and now a third. Grace had

had quite enough of it. There were ideas that needed to be expressed. Not those related to narrow interpretations of contract law or what constituted "reasonable expectation", but big, life-altering, soul-affirming ideas, the kind that couldn't be litigated in a courtroom but only in that rarified place within each individual's heart and mind where the artist claimed dominion. Her dominion. She wanted her goddamn money.

"It's mine as well as yours," she said. "Just because I don't work a traditional job doesn't mean you can hold me hostage."

"I'm not holding you hostage."

"I won't beg and scrape for every cent. You agreed when we got married that we would share everything, fifty-fifty, right down the middle."

"I'm not asking you to beg. It's just bad timing. There's nothing to split right now."

"Have you heard of the Power and Control Wheel?"

"Oh, come on, Grace…"

"Using economic abuse, using male privilege…"

"Male privilege? I'm the only one with a job! You don't even do any housework, the maid does all of that."

"*Minimizing.* That's three spokes, Stilty."

"What happened to all the money I gave you last week?"

"It's tied up, ok? You're not the only one with liquidity issues!"

"Look…" Stilton rifled through the mess on his desk until he located his cell phone. After some furious swiping and typing, he said, "I just put fifty dollars in your checking account."

"Fifty bucks?" said Grace. "What am I going to do with that?"

"Buy supplies, promotional materials. You know, just like you said."

"What about studio space?"

"Improvise, Grace. Do it at our place if you have to. What's all that square footage for if not to fill it with lasting memories?"

"Cute," said Grace, but Stilton could already hear the fight going out of her voice. He held the receiver away from his face and gave a relieved sighed.

"I suppose that's a plan," she said. "Oh, but Stilty, really, do give that case of yours a rest! You're going to give yourself hives."

"I appreciate your concern," he said, more warmly now that the end of the call was in sight. "Don't worry, once this is over we'll have so much money we'll never have to feel stress again."

"I hope so, dear. Ta!"

Stilton hung up the phone and turned back to his monitor, dismayed to see that the brief he had been struggling all morning to write had not miraculously finished itself. Would no one leave him in peace? If it wasn't Grace, it was this business with the Slocum kid. Wasn't there a better way to deal with death threats than naming some random schmo from the salesfloor as 'temporary CEO'? Whatever happened to hiring bodyguards? Stilton practiced his breathing. No sense in getting worked up over it. One way or another he was going to have to retain outside counsel to take the reins on his lawsuit. May as well accept it and focus on the immediate problems he could do something about.

Toggling between tabs, he pulled up a blank True North standard employment contract and began filling in the missing information. Nothing complicated about this one; he had done the same thing a hundred times before. Only the particulars about the end-date were unique. One way or another, Salvatore Slocum would be out of the executive suite in due time. Stilton just hoped the poor sap would survive long enough to collect his severance package.

Five

The roar of the recycling truck's engine was the first thing he heard. It bullied its way through the walls of his bedroom, pulling him back from the edge of sleep. He may yet have drifted off if not for the whine of the mechanical arm as it reached out to seize his bin. This was followed by a cacophony of falling metal, plastic, and glass as the arm hoisted the bin into the air, flipped it upside down and shook its contents free, like some mobster turning out the pockets of a deadbeat gambler.

Sal reached for his nightstand and groped around until he found his phone. The glare from the screen as he tapped it awake made him wince, as did the time it showed – 2:32 a.m. How was it acceptable to collect recycling at such an ungodly hour, he wondered? He would write to the Ashburg City Council about this. True, they hadn't responded to his previous seven letters regarding noise issues, but he had to be on surer footing this time. There had to be an ordinance for this sort of thing.

Now that he was fully awake a plethora of new sounds assaulted him. His white noise machine, rather than drown out, seemed to accentuate a series of ticks, thumps, snaps, and pops that crackled just outside the range of its incessant 'whooshing'. Sal pictured a menagerie of insects, rodents, burglars, and ghosts emboldened by the cover his machine provided, coming out of hiding to ply their trade in the open.

A gust of wind outside made the house shudder and creak, like an old man stretching his joints. A block away, the hiss of tires on wet pavement became briefly audible whenever a car passed by his street, then faded until it was subsumed by the din. Who was driving around at two-thirty in the morning on a Tuesday, he thought to himself? There was little enough to do in Ashburg during daylight hours.

With no hope of falling asleep again, Sal's thoughts turned to work and the orientation he had been given earlier that day. "*Orientation*", he thought, mentally placing quotation marks around the word. If the training he'd received had been comprehensive then he could definitively say that the job of chief executive required no special knowledge, skills, or abilities beyond that of being physically present in one's office. Mr. Leathers had, with alacrity and in painstaking detail, walked Sal through the rhythms of a typical day, which consisted mainly of checking his email, asking Sunny whether there was anything coming up on his calendar, and skimming the latest reports from the Analytics Department, a series of spreadsheets and graphs full of indecipherable terminology that even Leathers didn't pretend to understand.

"If there's anything you need to be concerned about, they'll highlight it red," he told Sal. "In that case just forward it over to Operations Support, tell them to take a look at it." Even the most cynical member of the working class would hardly credit that the guy upstairs could earn so much while doing so little.

The majority of Leathers' tutelage had centered around 'soft skills', a term he disdained. "Don't let anybody fool you, this is the *real* secret to being a leader," he said. The important thing was that others accept you as the guy in charge. "Carry yourself as if you own the room," he had explained. "Confidence is everything. Make firm decisions and stand by them, even when you're wrong. If someone asks you a question and you don't know the answer, don't be afraid to defer to an expert, but do it in a way that makes clear the question is beneath you, the kind of thing only functionaries concern themselves with. Remember, you're the big-picture guy." With his two index fingers Leathers traced a rectangle in the air between them. "Visualize it!"

Sal did as he was told, conjuring an image of himself seated at a heavy, oaken desk – a view of the Ashburg skyline visible through the floor-to-ceiling windows behind him – putting a gaggle of middle-managers in off-the-rack suits through their paces.

None of it bore a resemblance to the real True North – Leathers' actual desk was laminated plywood, there were no windows in his office, and Ashburg's 'skyline' was capped at seven stories due to zoning restrictions. Even the middle-managers he had imagined were not his actual coworkers but composites, as if all the business-wear mannequins from a JC Penney had come to life and worked their way up the corporate ladder. Sal realized at that moment that he had no idea what leadership looked like. All his ideas on the subject were variations of things he had seen on TV and in movies.

His confidence had started to flag then, but Leathers waved off his concerns. "It's easy," he said. "Watch." He picked up the phone and mumbled something to Sunny. A few minutes later a balding, bespectacled man shuffled into the office, clutching a stack of overstuffed file folders and wearing a sheepish expression.

"Now," Leathers said to Sal. "Tell him what to do."

"What?" said Sal.

"Go on," said Leathers. "Lead!"

Sal looked at the man, whose face shifted from nervous to bemused and back again as he tried to work out what was happening. "I don't even know who he is," said Sal. "What am I supposed to tell him?"

"That's Gene," said Leathers. "Gene, will you excuse us for a moment?"

Leathers beckoned to Sal to come closer, then closer still, until the two of them were huddled together in a corner of the room, whispering to one another like two children sharing a secret they didn't want a third child to hear. Just as he had earlier that day in Leathers' office, Sal felt the beginnings of a strange, vibrating sensation in his gut. He took a deep breath and tried to ignore it, hoping it would go away on its own.

"That's Gene," whispered Leathers. "He's in Accounting."

"Ok," said Sal. "What should I tell him to do?"

"You're thinking like a follower," said Leathers. "You're the leader, tell him whatever you want."

"But I don't know what he does." Sal suppressed a shudder as the vibration spread through his arms and legs. "How can I tell him what to do if I don't know what he's supposed to be doing?"

"He knows what he's supposed to be doing. And if he doesn't, he'll figure it out. The important thing is that whatever he ends up doing, he's doing it because he thinks that what *you* asked him to do."

Sal glanced over his shoulder. Gene – who had been craning his neck trying to hear what they were saying – quickly stood at attention, hugging the folders to his chest like a security blanket.

Stars danced in front of Sal's eyes. He took a moment to steady himself before turning back to Leathers. "He's afraid of me," he said.

"Of course he is," said Leathers. "To him, you're the guy in charge. Or *a* guy in charge, anyway. It's your job to cement that feeling. Every time he looks at you from this day forward, he should be thinking to himself, *That's the guy I need to worry about. That's the guy I need to keep happy.*"

Sal could feel beads of sweat bubbling up across his back and arms. He said a silent prayer that his clothes weren't staining through as he shifted his weight from one leg to the other. A crackling, itchy feeling like the pins and needles when a foot falls asleep crawled up and down the surface of his skin. Sal squirmed, alternately rubbing his fingers and scratching at his face and neck as the sensation jumped from place to place, as if his nerve endings were playing a game of whack-a-mole.

Leathers regarded him for a moment. "Or maybe I was mistaken," he said. "Maybe my gut was wrong about you. Maybe you're the type who's content to just coast along, doing the bare minimum for a modest wage. A loafer, trying to stay under the radar…"

"No sir!" Sal's voice was like an open palm to Leathers' face. It was the voice of a star quarterback about to lead his team onto the field for a game-winning drive. The abrupt change surprised him nearly as much as it did Leathers, who leaned back a few paces and studied him anew.

For a moment, all the discomfort and distress Sal had been feeling vanished. "No sir, quite the opposite, I look upon my work not only as a means to an end but a vehicle through which I can hone and perfect those intangible qualities that imbue a life with meaning and distinguish mankind from common beasts. To shirk one's duty to one's employer is to thumb one's nose at the great gift our Lord has provided us, which requires the exercise of responsibility to fully realize the benefits of self-awareness. I should sooner cast myself from polite society than be pulled along like driftwood by the honest labors of others."

As if a spirit that had possessed him suddenly passed out of his body, Sal shuddered and looked around. Even he wasn't sure where the words he had just spoken had come from, though he clearly remembered saying them.

"Good," said Leathers, a thin-lipped smile on his face. Almost immediately, the vibrations and nausea Sal had been feeling before started to return. His jaw stiffened and his teeth began to ache. A pulsating rhythm echoed through his head, as if someone were banging on his skull like a tom tom. More than anything he wanted to get away, to have a moment to himself to regroup before he lost control.

Breaking huddle with Leathers, Sal moved behind the desk and stood facing Gene. "Gene, is it?" he said. Gene nodded. "Well, Gene, what have you brought me there?" He spoke fluidly, worrying less about the words he was saying than that he said them without hesitation. He lowered the pitch of his voice, tossing in some staccato t's and accordion-stretched a's like a community theater actor channeling Tyrone Power.

"Well, I…" said Gene, before trailing off, staring at Sal with bovine eyes.

"The folders, Gene." Sal gestured. "Tell me about them."

"Folders?" Gene looked down at the folders in his arms and started, as if they had somehow gotten there without his knowledge. "These are the financial statements I always bring for Mr. Leathers to review. I've got our balance sheets, and our income and cash-flow statements for the last two quarters, along with…"

"I'm not *interested* in the last two quarters," said Sal. "I want to know where we're going. I want to know how to make True North the undisputed, number-one direct sales company in the country."

"But…I'm an accountant."

"Is that *all* you are?"

Gene stared, his lower lip protruding like the rim of a pitcher plant. It was a more existential question than he typically faced in these meetings.

"Let me tell you what I believe," said Sal. "I believe you're more than just a label. I believe that underneath this veneer of *accountant* you wear there lies a complex, multi-faceted individual with ideas and talents the rest of us – and maybe even you, yourself – can only guess at. Do you know what *synergy* is?"

"The fitness club?"

"The concept. The top organizations in the world get there by leveraging the untapped potential of their workforces. Why can't a mailroom clerk find efficiencies in our order processing workflow? Why can't an accountant create our next great marketing campaign?"

"Oh, I'm not very creative…"

"Are you a team player?"

"Team?" said Gene. "I mean…yes?"

"Good," Sal nodded. "When we each chart our own course, we're just lonely vessels adrift in a massive sea, but point our boats in the same direction and we become an armada."

"Like the Spanish Armada."

"Sure," said Sal.

"They were defeated by the English," said Gene. "But I suppose there's no accounting for weather. Or at least there wasn't in the 16th century."

"This is precisely the type of brainstorming that's going to get us to the next level." Sal came around from behind the desk and headed for the door, sweeping up Gene along the way. "I'm glad we had this talk. Now I want you to go out there and make me – make this organization – proud."

"I will, sir!" said Gene, as Sal shuttled him outside. Gene turned back as though to say something, but Sal had already shut the door behind him.

The sound of slow clapping came from across the room. "Very impressive," said Leathers. "Just the right balance of condescension and praise."

"I wasn't too harsh?"

"You have to tear down the person you are before you can build up the person you want to be." Leathers came forward and put a hand on Sal's shoulder. "True North instructional manual, Chapter 3, Part 5."

Sal felt the vibration – which had steadily ebbed throughout his conversation with Gene – begin to strengthen once more. "Do you mind if we take a break?" he said. "I'd like to use the restroom and take care of a few things."

"Not at all," said Leathers. "Let's adjourn for today. We can circle back tomorrow morning when Legal has all the paperwork prepared."

Sal offered a perfunctory goodbye as he hurried from the office. No sooner was he on the other side of the door than blessed relief washed over him – his jaw loosened, the pins and needles dissipated. By the time he made it back to his cubicle he was his old self again. All that remained was his confusion at what was happening to him. What was Leathers playing at? How could his life have changed so drastically since that morning? These thoughts consumed him the rest of the day, so much so that he didn't even offer an answer when Colleen asked him which former U.S. president would make the best ice hockey player.

Sal checked his phone again – 3:13 a.m. – then set it aside and lay staring up through the darkness at the faint impression of his ceiling fan. Could it be that Leathers was right about him, he wondered? Was there a natural leader buried somewhere inside him that needed only a little coaxing to come out?

Perhaps. But why was everything happening so quickly? Why was Leathers in such a hurry to leave that he would turn over his company to a sales rep off the floor instead of conducting a thorough search for a replacement? Did Sal even want to be CEO? Amidst all the confusion of the day he hadn't stopped to think about it. When he tried now, all he could think of was how tired he was. He adjusted his pillow, settled in, and stared at the back of his eyelids, listening to the lid of his recycling bin – left open by the truck – bang rhythmically against the side of the can.

<u>Six</u>

It was a roadside motel on the edge of the High Plains, the kind of place with a blinking neon sign shaped like an arrow out front. A long, low stucco building with a dozen numbered doors faced the road, while in the back a half-empty swimming pool gathered mildew. Empty plastic lawn chairs were scattered about the property, some of them clustered together and surrounded by discarded cigarette butts and half-empty beer cans, as if the occupants had been raptured mid-party.

Only two of the parking spots out front were occupied. Bagley pulled the Tercel into an empty space and killed the engine. The way he had felt when he'd left the Alamo Bar & Grill, he'd imagined driving straight through the night and the following day until he reached Ashburg. But the highways out west are long. Once the sun dips below the horizon and the natural scenery gets swallowed up by darkness there's not much to see, just miles and miles and miles of pavement unfurling in a straight line, bathed yellow by the glow of the headlamps.

Bagley's enthusiasm began to wane sometime around midnight. He pushed on until just after three, when the sight of a motel in the distance – glimpsed beneath drooping eyelids – killed off whatever remained of his resolve. 'The Drifter' was not a name that would draw most motorists in off the road, but the vacancy sign was lit, and for Bagley the promise of a bed was more than enough to overcome any issues with the branding.

He climbed out of the car and slumped toward the office, which jutted out from one end of the building like the base of a letter L. In fact, it was an 'Office/Lounge', as a carved wooden sign beside the entrance informed him. Upon entering, Bagley could find no evidence that a lounge existed, unless that was the name the owner had bestowed upon the pair of fraying recliners, drip coffee maker, and magazine-covered table that occupied one half of the room. To the left of the lounge was the front desk, behind which stood a woman who would have looked pretty good for eighty, but unfortunately, Bagley estimated, was probably closer to fifty. Over her shoulder a television that was nearly as old broadcast a grainy episode of Wheel of Fortune.

"What you want?" she said, when she caught sight of Bagley. Her rheumy eyes regarded him as one might a potentially rabid raccoon.

"A room," said Bagley.

"Here?"

"You got somewhere else I can stay?"

The woman frowned, but relaxed a bit. Apparently the armed robbers and serial killers around those parts didn't bother with pleasantries before getting down to business, thought Bagley.

The woman scanned an ancient ledger with yellowing paper, then half-turned and gestured toward a wooden rack with keys dangling from it. "Take your pick."

"What's the difference?" said Bagley.

"This here key that say one on it? That's for room one. And this here that say two? That's room two."

"What's the difference between room one and room two?"

"Room one is right over there." She pointed at the wall to Bagley's right. "Room two is one more down."

"What I mean is, is one room better than another? Is there one you'd recommend?"

The woman thought for a moment. "Depends how far down you want to be. If you want to be far down that a-way, pick a big number. You want to be up this way, pick a little number."

"Well, that is a choice," said Bagley. "Tell you what, give me something down there near my car." He nodded toward the window.

The woman adjudged the distance to the window, muttered some unpleasantries, and then staggered around from behind the desk to get a better look at where Bagley's car was parked. "That red bucket of bolts down there yours?"

"Bucket of bolts?!" Bagley's eyes goggled. "I'll have you know that there automobile has kept me in good stead for nearly two decades."

"It looks like one of them fry cartons from McDonald's."

"That is a vintage 1988 Toyota Tercel."

"Jap junk," she said.

"Madam, your prejudice is woefully outdated."

"What's that mean?"

"No one hates Japanese cars anymore."

"Well, I do."

"That's stupid."

"Who you callin' stupid?"

"I ain't calling you stupid, I'm saying you're saying a stupid thing."

"Well, that's just how I feel."

"Now listen…what's your name, sweetheart?"

"It sure as shit ain't sweetheart, Mac."

"Ain't you going to tell me?"

"*Irene*, if you must know."

"Irene, this is ludicrous. You're like one of them Japanese soldiers wandering around the jungle in the 1970s, still fighting Word War Two." He jerked a thumb toward the window. "You know how many miles that old girl out there's got on her?"

"Quite a few, by the looks of it."

"Three hundred and forty thousand! You ever heard of such a thing? That's Japanese engineering for you."

"What are you, the mayor of Tokyo or something?"

"You can ride that baby, pedal to the metal, all day and night, and the next time you start her up she'll purr like a kitten!"

"All right, all right, you love your car." Irene waved a hand at him, then took another look out the window. She squinted. "I'll put you in room seven."

"Sounds fine," said Bagley. He trailed after her as she hobbled back behind the desk. "I'm sorry I got a bit heated there. I've been on the road all night, and I'm all in but my shoestrings."

Irene grunted as Bagley forked over thirty dollars. She handed him a key attached to a black plastic oval emblazoned with the number '7'.

Bagley tipped his hat. "Thank'ee," he said, then pirouetted and moseyed out of the office and back down the length of the building to room seven. He paused outside the door for a moment, then continued on, all the way to room ten, which is where his car was actually parked. "Some guess," he grumbled, climbing back into the driver's seat and moving the Tercel down a few spots.

Once he had parked again, he grabbed his Italian leather saddlebag out of the back seat. He'd come across it years ago while browsing a Fingerhut catalog and was immediately smitten, believing it looked like something James Arness might have carried through the streets of Dodge City. Bagley liked to travel lightly, "free and loose" as he put it, like a wandering cowboy. His bag was just the right size for a toothbrush, a modestly sized firearm, and a single change of clothes. One change was all you needed, reasoned Bagley, a philosophy he had maintained until the third day of his trip, which he had spent inquiring after laundromats.

After a good deal of jiggling the key in the lock Bagley managed to open his room door. From where he stood on the threshold the bed, nightstand, and armchair he glimpsed through the darkness didn't look so bad. He only hoped he continued to feel that way when he turned on the lights. Feeling along the inside wall, he found the switch and flipped it up. Nothing happened. There was a second switch beside the first, so he tried that one. Again, the room remained dark.

Using his bag to prop open the door, Bagley went inside and tried turning on the table lamp next to the bed, twisting the switch once, twice, three times, before realizing it didn't have a bulb. He groped his way deeper into the room, past where the light from the parking lot reached, and tested the bathroom light – once more, nothing. A minute later he was back at the Office/Lounge, giving Irene a piece of his mind.

"What gives?" he said.

Irene frowned. "You again."

"I said what gives?"

"Now what the hell kind of question is that?"

"There aren't any lights in my room!"

"Sure there are. They just don't got any bulbs in 'em."

"What good's a light without a bulb?"

"Nothing," said Irene. "That's why bulbs are ten dollars extra."

"Ten dollars?!"

"Each."

"Boy, I tell you…" Bagley dug through his pockets. *"Where there's more of giving and less of buying,* my rear end." He found his wad of cash, counted out ten dollars and handed it over.

"Just one?" said Irene.

"I'll get by," said Bagley. "I ain't one to be chiseled."

"Where you going to put it?"

"The table lamp, I reckon."

"The overhead lamp would give you more coverage."

"I'm too tired to be climbing on chairs, fiddling around with fixtures."

"What about the bathroom?"

"What about it?"

"How are you going to see where to do your business?"

"I'll bring the table lamp with me."

"Hmph," Irene sniffed. "Just don't go dropping it in the bathtub, now."

"Scout's honor," said Bagley, holding up three fingers.

"At least not before seven," said Irene. "That's when my shift ends. I don't wanna be the one hauling your flabby behind out of that clawfoot, understand?"

What a morbid old broad, thought Bagley, as Irene dug a bulb out of a cardboard box beneath the counter. He took it from her, put it to his forehead and flashed a salute before returning to his room. As he approached the door, he noticed a blue Volvo parked a few spaces down from his Tercel. Had that been there before, he wondered? He didn't recall seeing it. Must have been an early check-in, he reasoned, out soaking up whatever nightlife Route 104 might have to offer.

Bagley fought with the lock for a minute or two, but eventually managed to pop the door open and slip inside. As he made his way over to the bed the door swung shut behind him, plunging him into near-total darkness. He felt around until he found the table lamp, then managed to locate the socket and screw in the bulb. Nothing happened the first time he turned the switch. The second turn produced a dim, orange glow, and with the third turn the room lit up to the furthest corner.

"You got something that belongs to me," said a voice behind him.

Bagley turned and stumbled at the same time, falling backwards to sit on the edge of the bed. Between him and the door stood Elmie, a long-barreled Colt revolver with an ivory grip and floral scroll engraving in her hand. The barrel was pointed at his chest.

"Christ, woman," he said, between labored breaths. "I've got a pacemaker, you know. You nearly gave me a heart attack."

"Good way to save a bullet," said Elmie.

"That's my gun."

"Tit for tat."

"I don't know what that means." Bagley held his hands up at shoulder level. He could feel himself slipping off the bed and tried to shift his weight, but Elmie shook the Colt at him and froze him in his tracks. "I'm going to fall on my ass if I don't move, Elmie," he said.

"You remembered my name, at least," she sneered.

"Is this about your ID?"

Elmie didn't respond. Bagley caught her eye, flexed the fingers on his right hand, and raised his eyebrows. A moment later, he began inching his hand toward his back pocket, maintaining eye contact the entire time. Elmie kept the gun trained on him, but there were no more threatening gestures this time, which Bagley took as having permission to continue. He slipped his fingers into the pocket and pulled out the ID. "This what you're looking for?"

"What I'm looking for," she said, "is an explanation for why a man would play with the emotions of a vulnerable woman who's been hurt too many times to count just to steal a worthless piece of plastic."

"It wasn't like that."

"Yeah?" Elmie's voice rose in pitch. "Exactly what part am I misremembering? As I recall it, a charming man in a cowboy hat was awkwardly flirting with me at the bar, giving me his best *aw shucks* routine until I let my guard down, then took off the minute I left the room without so much as a goodbye." As she spoke the last few words, her voice quavered. Her eyes became round and watery, and she had to clear her throat before continuing. "Or am I getting confused with one of the other times a guy broke my heart?"

"Oh, Elmie…" Bagley stopped and squinted. His mouth remained frozen mid-sentence, stretched out and narrowly parted like a vending machine coin slot. His eyes bounced around the room – left, right, and back again – as they tended to whenever he was thinking something through. "Jeezum crow, you followed me all the way here?"

"Boy, you are a sharp one. I suppose I can take comfort in the fact that I fell prey to one of the great minds of our age."

"Now don't get snippy. It's a long drive is all I'm saying."

"Yeah, it sure was. Exactly what is it that's got you swiping expired ID cards and driving across two states in the middle of the night?"

"I got a score to settle."

"Looks like we have something in common, then."

"Elmie, listen to me." Bagley stood up off the bed. Elmie raised the barrel of the gun, but she didn't flinch, nor did she back away. "When I stopped by the Alamo it was with the sole intention of grabbing a quick bite to eat and being on my way. I had no idea that a beautiful woman would strike up a conversation with me…"

"More sweet talk," she snarled.

"Just listen. What I'm saying is that I've been wronged, and when that happens I get a one-track mind about things. It never occurred to me that I might be leading you on. All I knew was that I fell into a bit of luck, and in my experience when that happens you have to chase it."

"And who was it that wronged you, exactly?"

"You remember how I told you I tried True North? How they scammed me?"

"Yeah, and?"

"I want my refund."

Elmie stared at him. "That's it?"

Bagley nodded.

"So why not just call and ask for a refund?" she said.

"I tried. No dice."

"And now you're driving across the country to, what, beat it out of them? Fifty lousy bucks?"

"It's not about the money."

"Well, what is it about?"

"It's about not getting stepped on anymore." Something changed in Bagley's voice as he spoke these words, a crack through which years of suppressed emotions began to seep. It was enough to stun Elmie out of her anger. For the first time, she lowered the Colt. "You're serious," she said.

"Yes, ma'am."

"You want to tell me about it?"

And so he did, spinning a yarn of hardship and woe to put the saddest cowboy songs to shame. From the very beginning people had been abandoning him. His parents had given him up for adoption as a baby.

He had no memory of what they looked or sounded like. His adoptive parents had also given him up, finding him to be "not worth the trouble". By age six he was in an orphanage, at which point he began his carousel ride through a succession of foster homes. The longest he had remained in one place was four months, and only because his foster mother at the time had found a way to make money soliciting donations to cover the costs of his non-existent 'cancer treatments'.

Still without a permanent home at age 18, the orphanage had handed him twenty dollars and punted him out onto the streets. Somehow, through a combination of determination and luck he had managed to beat the odds and scrape together a life for himself. He found a job that – while not exactly fulfilling – paid enough that he could afford his bills and a tiny studio apartment in the bad part of town. Years of scrimping and saving allowed him to work his way up to a bigger place in a better neighborhood, but what remained elusive was any sort of meaningful connection to the people around him. His boss did not respect him. His coworkers barely acknowledged his existence. Women paid him no attention; he had never been in a serious relationship before. He had no close friends, and of course, no family. Even the casual acquaintances he made during his daily routine – the cashier at the coffee shop, the mailman, the owner of the grocery stand beside his building – only tolerated him, at best. He had managed to survive, and for what? He was all alone.

What kicked off his obsession with self-improvement he could no longer remember. Was it the hypnotism treatments or the juice cleanses, the spinning classes or the real estate courses, the Toastmasters or the Promise Keepers? Sometimes it felt that for as long as he had been alive, he had been trying to fix himself. In that way, there was nothing exceptional about True North. It had simply been the straw that broke the camel's back.

"When I took out that compass," said Bagley, "and it was pointing directly at me, when I *know* I'm as mixed up as a twice-used puzzle, it was more than I could take. I'm just looking for some answers, I suppose, but to even ask those sorts of questions marks you as a sucker. That's just the world we live in."

"Are you sure you weren't just standing to the north of it?" said Elmie.

"What?" said Bagley.

"The compass. How do you know you weren't just standing to the north of it, and so it happened to point at you?"

"Cause I walked around in circles. Lookit…" Bagley crossed the room to where his bag was lying on the floor. Elmie made no movement to stop him, watching as he knelt down and dug around inside, eventually producing the compass. He held it out where she could see and began revolving around it, slowly, like a very large planet around a tiny sun. Wherever he moved, the needle followed.

"See that?" he said. "What a hunk of junk." He tossed the compass onto the bed. "To be honest, I don't even care so much about the refund. I just wanted someone to give a damn, to say they were sorry."

"And that's what you're going to do when you get there?" said Elmie. "Ask them to apologize?"

"No, I'm going to make them." Involuntarily, his eyes moved toward the gun.

"I see." Elmie was silent a moment. "You know, even if that ID you swiped from me were still active – which I can assure you, it isn't – I didn't work in the headquarters building anyway. What in the world were you planning to do with it?"

"Don't know," Bagley shrugged. "I guess I just figured I'd think of something."

"Well, I can solve half your problem."

"How's that?"

"Even the bozos a place like True North hires to work security can probably tell that's not your picture on that card."

"And?"

"Now you've got the genuine article." Elmie held a hand up beside her face and grinned, like a catalog model.

"What are you saying?"

"I'm coming with you."

Bagley nearly collapsed onto the bed again. He tried to say something that would capture the mixture of shock, joy, and embarrassment he felt, but nothing would come. Instead, he stood by mutely while Elmie filled the void.

"I know what it's like to be abandoned," she said. "Like I said, I've had my heart broken more than once. Maybe that sounds trite compared to what you've been through, but it's more complicated than that. Let me explain…

"I was engaged once. I was very young, and very, very naïve, but I didn't know that at the time. I thought that because I was poor and had seen some of the rougher side of life that I was invulnerable to the sorts of silly crushes that made more-sheltered girls throw everything away and go chasing after the first guy who told them they were pretty. Then I met someone and fell in love.

"He was a few years older than me, tall, with this beautiful golden-brown hair he wore slicked back to keep it from standing on end. I was at the ice cream stand when he and two of his buddies got into line behind me. Already my guard was up. Who ever heard of grown men going to an ice cream stand? They were carrying on, shoving and laughing and making a scene. Every so often they'd check me out, then shoot each other a look when I caught them. Like I said, my guard was up. I knew what they were up to. There wasn't a girl over the age of twelve in my hometown who didn't know what a group of guys like that were after.

"Eventually, one of them said something to me. Not my guy, one of the others. I don't remember the exact words, only that it was as crude as you'd expect. I pretended not to hear, refused to turn around. They laughed of course, and I felt that shiver up my spine, the one that always came when I realized that my silent prayers of being ignored and left alone were not going to be answered. I thought about walking away, but fuck them, I wanted my ice cream.

"I could still hear them back there as I got up to the counter, talking to each other under their breath and tittering like a bunch of schoolgirls. I don't know if I appreciated the fact that they felt enough shame to keep their comments to themselves, or if I looked down on them for not having the guts to speak up and let everyone hear what kind of people they really were. Anyway, I ordered my ice cream, and as I'm walking away I give it a lick to keep it from dripping on my hand. Of course, that got them going. *Told you she knows what she's doing,* one of them said, or something to that effect. The thing is, I sort of did. I was seventeen, I had slept with guys before. More than one. Somehow, that made what he said even more embarrassing.

"Anyway, I've got my ice cream now, so there's no reason to stick around. I start walking away, when I feel a hand on my arm. It's a big hand, and strong. It's not squeezing me or anything, just lying there, but even so I can tell that if it tightened its grip there would be no way I could free myself unless it decided to let me go.

"I freeze. Now that shiver that was in my spine is everywhere. I'm trembling, my whole body is tense. My mind starts racing, trying to come up with plans for what to do if this thing starts going bad. *Why won't they just leave me alone,* I'm thinking to myself. Then a voice says, "Hey, wait a minute," and all my fears melt away. I turn around, and it's my guy, Jim – *Jimmy,* as his friends called him, but I always called him Jim. Jimmy sounded too much like a little boy's name, and besides, I didn't want to share any part of him with those other men.

"You're probably wondering what he said next to get past my defenses and win me over. Fact is, it was nothing special. I can't even remember the exact words. Something like, "Don't let those guys bother you," as if he hadn't been doing the same thing just ten seconds earlier. Again, I wasn't stupid. I'd seen that game before – a group of guys harass a girl, make her feel uncomfortable so that one of their buddies can step in and play the hero. Probably that's what Jim and his friends were up to, but at the time I didn't care. He was the handsomest guy I had ever seen, and his voice sounded so sincere. I figured, why not? Like I said, it wasn't my first time around the block. If he used me and took off, so what? Once you've been through the ringer a couple of times you realize it isn't so bad. At least, that's what I thought.

"I won't go into every last detail of our relationship. It was the usual stuff – guy makes a few gallant gestures to show he's not like 'other men', girl gets drunk on flattery and attention, and before you know it they're a couple. It wasn't long after my eighteenth birthday that I got pregnant. No one I knew back then was on the pill, and Jim whined and moaned about wearing condoms. I loved him, so of course I caved. That's how our son, James Jr. – 'little Jimmy' – came about.

"Friends of mine, if you could call them that, kept warning me that Jim would leave me for sure now that a baby was on the way. Some told me I should marry him as soon as possible. Others said I should get an abortion. That way, no matter what happened between me and Jim I would still have my whole life ahead of me. I wasn't so sure. Not that I was worried what others might think – like any small town, mine had its share of moralizers and gossips, but our community was too poor not to accept abortion as at worst a necessary evil. It wasn't practical considerations either. The nearest clinic was two hours away, but Jim had a job and a car, and I knew he would pay for it if only to get himself out of a jam. All I can say is that it just didn't feel right. There's no logical reason I can give for feeling that way. Maybe it was the hormones doing their work.

"I decided I wasn't going to propose to Jim. Let him take the initiative, if that was something he really wanted. Weeks and months passed. He never did ask me to marry him, but he didn't leave either. When I had a doctor's appointment, he would take me. When I needed something from the store, he would buy it for me. We went along like that, day after day after day, going through the motions of building a life together. I never pushed the issue. The longer things went on like that the less I worried about it, and besides, I didn't want to jinx what we had.

"Inertia has a way of making decisions when people can't. When the birth finally came and Jim was there for it, I figured that was it. Married or not, it felt like he was in it for the long haul. Once I'd had a chance to hold the baby for a while, the nurses picked him up and handed him to Jim. Watching him holding his son like that, I knew I had made the right choice.

Things were going to work out. For the next year or so that continued to be true.

"Jim had this crazy idea that we should pack up the family and go on a cross-country trip. This was right around the time James Jr. was turning one. A guy from Jim's work had a camper he wasn't using, and he told Jim we could borrow it for the summer. It sounded crazy to me, dragging a toddler along on a months-long road trip, sleeping cooped up together in the back of a van in whatever parking lot or campground we happened to find. What was the point, when little Jimmy wouldn't even remember it?

"Jim didn't care. Once the idea entered his head there was no dissuading him. He had already worked something out with his boss to take the time off. The opportunity might never come up again. To be honest, I always knew we would end up going. As wary as I was, I was also damned sick of staring at the same four walls for the better part of a year, not to mention the same damn town the entire nineteen years I'd been alive. It didn't take much to bring me over to Jim's way of thinking. I wanted to see a little of the world myself, and besides, it made me feel good to be able to give him something, a way of saying thanks for sticking by me when I knew he could have left anytime he wanted.

"We left in the middle of June. I still remember that first day, pulling out of the driveway, all the anxiety and excitement and promise of what was to come. I felt giddy, like I'd been sipping champagne.

"We headed east to start, through Appalachia and up into New England. Spent some time in the mountains in Vermont and New Hampshire, then turned south and went down the eastern seaboard. Jim was dead set on spending a week in the Smokies, so when we reached the Carolinas we turned west. We had been on the road about three weeks at that point. Everything was going perfectly. Even James Jr. had never been so well behaved. Sure, he fussed now and again, but he seemed to be having the time of his life, bumbling around in the grass whenever we stopped for the night. It was on that trip that he took his first real steps, trying to get a closer look at a squirrel that kept buzzing around an oak tree that was next to the camper, nibbling at acorns. He'd toddle after it, lose his balance and fall on his butt, then put his hand up to his face like this, right along the side of his nose and mouth like he was about to tell someone a secret. He always did that when he was confused or upset. It's one of the things I remember about him most." She paused for a moment, growing wistful. "But he kept getting back up and trying again. I remember feeling really proud.

"Anyway, we were driving through North Carolina, and we stopped off at a state park somewhere in the Piedmont. It was a pretty place, and we were in no great hurry. We decided to spend a night or two. There were plenty of campsites open. We paid the fee, got set up, and then spent an hour or so goofing around with James Jr. It was late afternoon, so Jim decided to get some firewood. They had wood already chopped and dried back at the ranger station that you could buy for five dollars a bundle, but Jim wouldn't hear of it. Why waste the money when there's free wood all around us, he'd say. I think he just liked the excuse to go off on his own and wander for a bit. I didn't mind. We were together nearly every minute of every day. People need some time apart. Absence makes the heart grow fonder, they say.

"I don't know how long it was before I started to worry. Normally, when he went to gather wood, he was rarely gone for more than thirty minutes at a time, even if just to drop off what he'd collected so far before heading back out again. I tried busying myself so I wouldn't look at my watch every five minutes, but eventually I couldn't take it anymore. I glanced down and saw an hour and a half had passed. Still, I told myself not to panic. I fed James Jr., changed the bedding in the camper. All the while the light outside was growing dimmer. At first I thought I'd lost track of time and that night was falling, but when I stuck my head outside I saw a wall of clouds, huge and dark, rolling in from the south. Finally, I let myself look at my watch again – nearly three hours since he'd first set out.

"I wasn't sure what to do. The ranger station was a mile from our campsite. No sooner had I made up my mind to put James Jr. in the carrier and walk over there to report Jim missing than the rains came – just a drizzle at first, but then a deluge, pounding like fists on the camper roof. Thunder was booming in the distance and moving closer. There was no way I could have driven. It would have taken me forever to undo all the hookups and get the camper ready to go, even without the storm. Besides, what if he came back while I was gone? I didn't want to strand him there in the rain, with lightning moving in and nowhere to take shelter.

"So, I did what people always do when they don't know what the right decision is – nothing. I hunkered down, kept Jimmy entertained until he fell asleep, then curled up on the bed and worried and prayed until at some point I fell asleep myself.

"When I woke up it was the following morning. The storm had passed and there was sun pushing in through the curtains. I burst out of the camper and looked around. No Jim. This time I did make the trek to the ranger station, Jimmy crying and fussing the entire way. Once I'd explained the situation, they sent a team out to look for him. The local cops were called in, Fish and Game…they even brought in a helicopter. He was nowhere to be found. Jimmy and I stayed at the campground for three more days while the search continued, but eventually we were told that they were going to have to start scaling back, and that it was being reclassified from a rescue to a recovery mission.

"It's funny how quickly your convictions can change. At first, I was adamant that I would never budge from that campground so long as Jim was still out there somewhere. But days go by. Nothing happens. There's this terrible stasis…but then maybe that's not the right word for it. Things do change. The way the police and rescue teams speak to you isn't quite as sympathetic as it once was. Your food and supplies start running low. You realize a part of you wishes you were home, around familiar things and people, with a familiar bed to sleep in. It isn't that you care one bit less about the person who's gone missing. Maybe it's just your body's way of telling you that life must go on, no matter what. That's basically what the Chief of Police told me – 'You've got a little one to look after. Why don't you take him home? There's nothing more you can do here.' And he was right, as awful as it made me feel. Especially awful, as I felt in my heart that I hadn't done anything at all.

"And so, I went. Packed up the camper, turned it around – it took about a dozen tries, *God* how I hated driving that thing – pulled out on the highway and headed west. The drive back took no time at all. Before I knew it I was home, in the apartment Jim and I had been renting together, surrounded by all those familiar things. There was some initial relief at being back, where I knew the routine. Now there was only one big thing I needed to worry about. 'We'll keep in touch and let you know the moment there's any news,' the police had told me before I left. They never told me what would happen if there wasn't any news. *That* I would have to learn for myself, day after agonizing day.

"You don't just wake up one day and realize your life will never be the same. At least I didn't. It's a gradual thing, a series of small changes that you accept as temporary until before you know it they've become permanent.

"I say *small changes*, but some are bigger than others. Like when it became clear that I couldn't afford to keep us in the apartment anymore. Jim was the only one working at the time. He paid the rent, all the bills. Our town didn't have a daycare. If you needed someone to watch your kids, you asked your family. Only my family wanted nothing to do with me. What little family I had. My father took off before I was born, and my mother had always resented me, both as a reminder of the man that had left her high and dry and as an unwanted obligation getting in the way of finding a new man.

"When she found out I was pregnant she was positively gleeful. Not because she was going to be a grandma, but because now she could look down on me the way she thought everyone was always looking down on her. She called me stupid for getting knocked up, and she took every opportunity to run down Jim's character (when she wasn't trying to flirt with him, that is) and tell me it was only a matter of time before he left me. When I came back from our trip by myself, in my mother's eyes it vindicated every awful prediction she had ever made. Not only did she refuse to lift a finger to help her grandson, but she openly gloated over my bad fortune. Things kept getting worse. Our utilities got cut off. An eviction notice got posted on the door. That's when I made the hardest decision I'd ever had to make…"

For the first time during her long soliloquy, Elmie fell silent. Bagley had been listening raptly throughout, and it took him a moment to shake out of his reverie. "Well?" he said. "What was the decision?"

Elmie's gaze bored a hole through the floor between them. She gnawed at her lower lip. "I'm not sure I can bring myself to say it. I'm afraid what you'll think of me."

"What I'll think of you?" said Bagley. "A few minutes ago you had a gun pointed at me. Are you really that worried about my opinion?"

"Yes," she said. "Given what you told me about your past."

"My past?" Bagley squinted in confusion, but no sooner had he asked the question than it dawned on him what she meant. "You gave your son up for adoption, didn't you?"

Elmie nodded. As if a switch had been flipped, tears welled up in the corners of her eyes, winding their way down the contours of her face in narrow streams. "I didn't know what else to do," she said.

"Hey," said Bagley, leaning forward to clasp her hand. "I don't blame you, ok? It's not my place to judge. Life's tough enough on its own, let alone when you're a teenager trying to raise a kid by yourself." He left her for a moment to grab a tissue off the nightstand, then gave it to her. "Did you ever find out what happened to Jim?" he asked.

Elmie shook her head. "No," she said, dabbing at her face, "I never did. Sometimes it feels like a part of me will stay living there forever, replaying that day over and over, that moment when he told me he'd be right back and I watched him wave goodbye and disappear into the woods…"

Seven

They had been playing with Junior when Jim noticed it was past four-thirty. He glanced over his shoulder at the firepit; nearly dinner time, and they still hadn't gathered any wood. They could cook something on the stove, he supposed, but what was the point of camping without a nice fire to sit around in the evening? He had to go soon. It got dark early in the forest.

"Be back in a bit," he said to Elmie. "Going to grab some firewood." He was up to the tree line before he realized she hadn't answered. That wasn't like her. A flicker of fear passed through him, and he looked back. Elmie was right where he'd left her, sitting cross-legged on their big outdoor blanket coaxing Junior to try to stand up. Their eyes met, and he gave a little wave before trudging off through the trees.

Not far into the woods he came upon a ridge, on the other side of which was a shallow basin with a creek meandering through the center. He scuttled down and stood for a moment at the water's edge, listening to the sounds of nature. Now that he could no longer see the camper behind him or hear Elmie making babytalk with Junior, a tension he hadn't even known was there began to dissipate from his back and shoulders. He held himself a bit straighter, breathed easier. For a few moments he just stood there with his eyes closed, basking in the sensation, but it didn't take long for the guilt to begin seeping in. There was something improper, he felt, about enjoying being apart from one's family. That didn't make him move any faster. He could live with the guilt if that was the price he had to pay for moments like this.

Things had not turned out as he had imagined they would when he'd stepped into line behind that pretty young girl at the ice cream stand the year before. One minute he'd been tossing out hopeful lines, not expecting to get back much more than a few dirty looks, and the next he was a father with a family to take care of.

Not that he was unhappy with his new life – far from it. But the rapidity with which his circumstances had changed left him feeling disoriented at times. Would he still have chosen to talk to Elmie if he had known where it would lead him? Possibly not. Maybe, he reflected, that was why life didn't offer such choices. Sometimes you just had to roll the dice and live with the consequences.

Jim crossed the creek at a shallow point and moved deeper into the forest, scanning the floor for dead wood. He had been told at the ranger station that they had crews out cutting down and sectioning dead trees, and that anyone was welcome to haul out the chunks and use them for fuel. So far, he hadn't come across any. There were branches scattered everywhere, though, some of them large. Most of the ones he picked up and examined he ended up discarding – too damp, too green. As he was in no hurry to get back, he could afford to be picky.

By the time his arms were full nearly an hour had passed. Jim looked up from the floor to take stock of his surroundings. He wasn't entirely sure which direction he'd come from. There had been a vague sense that he'd been keeping track of the topography as he'd wandered along, mentally cataloguing anything notable to use like a trail of breadcrumbs to find his way back. It was only now that he realized how little attention he'd actually been paying. None of the markers he remembered were anywhere in sight.

At least he could still see clearly, he thought to himself. Despite the advancing hour the woods were brighter than they had been when he'd first set out. The sun seemed to be angling in beneath the forest canopy, like someone leaning down to shine a flashlight underneath a bed. That only made sense if there was a clearing of some sort nearby. Jim headed due west, following the sunlight, hoping to find a park trail or fire access road he could take back to his campground.

When at last he reached the break in the trees it was not a road that greeted him, but a steep cliff abutting a waterfall. From another part of the forest, across a horseshoe divide, water poured out from beneath the trees and cascaded down a series of boulders to a pool far below (at least a hundred feet, Jim estimated) that formed the head of a river.

As eager as he was to find his way back to the camper, Jim couldn't help but appreciate the beauty of the falls – the incessant rumble of water against the stones, the mist rising up to catch the sun, creating thin rainbow-colored streamers that undulated toward the sky. He stood there for a moment taking it all in and gazing down the length of the gorge that the river had carved out, tracing its path until the point where it disappeared around an escarpment a mile or so to the south. It was such an idyllic scene that it took a while before he noticed the wall of black clouds advancing toward him in the distance, rolling and churning like the leading edge of an avalanche. Lightning strikes deep within its interior caused it to flicker up and down its mass, making it look as if a massive swarm of fireflies had taken to the sky.

For the first time, Jim felt a sense of urgency. He was no survivalist, but he had spent enough time in the woods to know that if he followed the source of the waterfall upstream it would have to lead him somewhere, perhaps even to the creek he had come across not far from his campsite. With no better plan in mind, he set about following the curve of the horseshoe – staying as close as he dared to the cliff's edge, retreating deeper into the woods only when the terrain required it – until at last he reached the mouth of the waterfall and the river that supplied it.

It was every bit a river, many times wider and deeper than any body of water he'd encountered on his hike thus far. His little creek was likely just a tributary, possibly one of many. He wondered if he'd know which one to branch off and follow when the time came. Or perhaps he should just stay with the river, he thought, see where it led him. There was a greater chance he'd find people that way, maybe someone who could give him a ride or at least shelter until the storm passed. He pushed those thoughts aside; it was a problem for later. The important thing now was to start moving.

He was just about to set off when something on the rocks near the lip of the waterfall caught his eye. Several things, in fact. Moving closer to investigate, he found a wallet and a pair of hiking boots sitting near each other, arranged precisely. Jim scanned the river and surrounding woods, then leaned out over the rocks and felt a flutter of vertigo as he traced the water's path down the side of the cliff. Could the owner have gone swimming and been swept over the edge, he wondered? Could they have jumped? Taking one more look around and seeing no one, he picked up the wallet and opened it, but found few answers there – the cash and credit card slots were empty, and there was no driver's license or other identification. It looked like a robbery, but then why leave the wallet sitting there so conspicuously? What about the shoes? And if it were a suicide, why take the money and leave the wallet? Why take off your shoes before you jump? Jim couldn't make sense of it.

A rumble of thunder, much closer now, shook him from his thoughts. He slipped the wallet into his pocket. Once he found his way back he would contact the police and turn it in, let them figure out what had happened here.

A gust of wind rustled the trees. A moment later, Jim felt the first drops of rain strike his arms and face. Hopping down from the rocks, he took what shelter he could along the tree line and scrambled upriver, moving as quickly as he dared along the narrow banks.

The sun that had provided such an unexpected respite just minutes ago was now swallowed up by the storm clouds, plunging the landscape into darkness that seemed to descend all at once, as if the boundary between day and night were a bright-line that had just been crossed. Jim stumbled and groped his way through the gloom, eager to press on yet fearful of what each step might bring.

The rain – until then just a pitter-pattering on the leaves above Jim's head – became a downpour, announcing itself with a dull roar, like a slumbering attack dog suddenly roused to consciousness. Now there was no escape. Even as he pressed deeper into the interior of the woods he could find no shelter. The rain pummeled the branches, shoving them rudely aside on its journey to the ground. Worse, the lightning strikes were getting closer. One momentarily lit up the woods like someone flipping on the lights in a darkened room; Jim half expected his friends and family to leap out from behind the trees wearing party hats and yell "Surprise!". Instead, a massive '*boom!*' shook the earth beneath his feet. Jim felt his knees buckle and reached out to steady himself. Now he adopted the opposite strategy, leaving the cover of the forest and hewing as closely as he could to the river's edge. He would get drenched no matter what he did, but the last place he wanted to be when lightning struck was surrounded by trees.

He continued on that way for some time – to Jim, it felt like an hour or more, though in reality was only minutes – until eventually his path was blocked by a stone outcropping, a wall of granite tens of feet tall that jutted into the water and formed the right bank of the river for as far as he was able to see. His only way forward was to backtrack a short distance, enter the woods and circle around to see if there was a path that would let him ascend the rocks. However, he could see that the river curved away to his left up ahead. It was unclear whether he'd be able to keep it in sight from the top of the cliff, or if the terrain would carry him in another direction, force him deeper into the woods where he'd become disoriented all over again. All the while the rain continued to pelt him, a million tiny punches to his face and body, making it impossible to concentrate.

As he looked around for an idea, he caught sight of what appeared to be a cave along the opposite riverbank. In reality it was more of an overhang, a few large stones protruding like a shelf from the upper part of the slope to form a sort of roof. It wasn't much, but it promised shelter from the rain. Moreover, where the current had been raging closer to the falls, here it moved at a relative crawl, slowed considerably by the bend up ahead. A fallen tree not far from where he stood covered a good deal of the distance to the other side, and there were enough rocks showing above the water that attempting a crossing seemed like the best idea. The worst that could happen was that he fell, Jim reasoned, and he could hardly get any wetter than he already was. He would spend the night there, wait out the storm, then work his way back in the light of day.

He leapt from rock to rock, picturing Elmie waiting for him back at the camper. She would be terrified, of course, imagining him being mauled by some wild animal or lying in a broken heap at the bottom of a cliff. He felt guilty for getting himself into this situation, but also a little giddy, imagining her reaction when he turned up safe and sound.

Perhaps it was selfish of him, he thought, as he made the longest and most difficult jump over to the tree, crouching as he landed and grasping the trunk with his hands and knees. Still, he relished the reception he knew he would get once the yelling was out of the way and Junior had been put to bed. Their love life hadn't been the same since their son had been born, but if anything would reignite the spark between them it would be his miraculous escape from the jaws of death.

Jim chuckled as he eased himself to his feet – legs quivering like a newborn fawn's – and began inching his way down the length of the trunk. Elmie had told him once that the only thing men cared about was sex. He'd argued with her about it at the time, but he had to admit he wasn't doing his side much credit at the moment. But then, he reflected, it wasn't sex he was fixated on – it was Elmie. She was always what his thoughts turned to whenever she wasn't near. That part hadn't changed since the first day they had met.

He thought back to the question he'd asked himself beside the creek earlier on, if he would still have talked to Elmie that day at the ice cream stand if he had known how things would turn out. It was a ridiculous question, he now realized. He couldn't have stopped himself from talking to her no matter what he had known then, even if it was destined that she would leave him one day and break his heart. Because he loved her. He had known it from the moment he had seen her walking away and had rushed forward, instinctively, to take her arm and tell her to wait. The way she had turned around to look at him with those round, frightened eyes had been like a dagger to his heart, and he had vowed in that instant to do everything he could to make sure she never felt frightened again. He supposed he had failed in that today, running off the way he had and getting lost. Still, he would make it up to her. And if he screwed up again, he would make up for that too. He'd spend the rest of his life proving he was worthy of the gift she had given him that day, when her eyes had finally softened and she had asked him to walk her home.

He could picture those eyes now, plain as day. They were the last thing he saw before the world dissolved into white light and ozone.

****

Thoughts piled up one upon the other, like train cars barreling into the side of a mountain-

I'm wet. I'm lying down. It feels sandy against my cheek. I hear leaves rustling. The breeze is cold. I should get up…no use. Can't seem to move. My arms and legs are there. I can sense them. The feeling is coming back. They're beginning to ache. Just lie here, listen to the water. The pain is not so bad. What's that smell? Burning cables? Birds are singing. Are there people around? Am I alone? Muscles are tingling. I can wiggle my toes now. My head is throbbing. I want to open my eyes, but I'm scared. Just lie here a minute, there's no rush. Everything in its time…

Eventually he did open his eyes. The influx of light made him wince, but after a moment's adjustment he saw that he was lying flat on his stomach on a sandy deposit by the side of a river. With considerable effort he lifted himself onto his hands and knees, then rolled over into a sitting position. Now he could see that he was in a densely wooded area. Towering stands of oaks, maples, and pines jockeyed with one another for the sun's rays. The river at his feet stretched away into the distance in both directions, the water gliding past without origin or destination.

The man was not at all surprised at his surroundings. Where else would he be, after all? And yet, when he tried to decide what to do next, where he should go, it necessarily made him consider why he was where he was. It was here that things became fuzzier.

Try as he might he could not construct the chain of events that had placed him in this forest, beside this river, on this particular day. This led naturally to the even more disturbing realization that he could not construct a chain of events that stretched back beyond the moment just minutes ago when he had awoken on the sand. Only one prior memory remained, if one could even call it a memory – a flash of light, blinding, ephemeral, that rose unbidden whenever he tried to plumb his past. Though he knew intellectually that this was not how things were supposed to be, he was oddly accepting of the situation, the way others accept that they cannot remember the moment of their birth. *I know who I am*, he thought, before realizing with distress that he could not put a name to himself.

Reaching for his pockets felt like a humiliating surrender, but anything was better than the creeping sense of dislocation this discovery had caused him. The memories would return, of that he was certain, and he was just as confident he could get by without them in the meantime. His sense of self was intact – that intrinsic feeling that '*I am me*' – but without a name he could not place himself in the world; nor, he knew, would others accept him as such. They would rush to name him themselves, as quickly as possible and according to their own whims. Without a name he was little more than an apparition or dream, something beyond language, like a shape without dimensions.

There was a sense of relief, then, when he discovered the wallet in the back pocket of his jeans.

He took it out and thumbed through it, but to no avail – it was empty. He was cursing his bad luck and about to put the wallet back when his eye caught the tiny letters stitched along the outer seam, by the bill compartment – Burton Leathers. He closed his eyes and allowed the name to rattle around in his brain, waiting to see if it would adhere. "Burt Leathers," he then said out loud, testing the feel of it on his tongue. He said it a second and third time, letting it vibrate against his eardrums.

Yes, he thought at last, *there's something familiar here. I am Burt Leathers.*

Now the man had a name.

His next concern was finding his way back to civilization. He may not have been able to remember what had brought him to this place, but he understood well enough that he had to leave. He was wet, and he was tired. Hunger pangs clawed at his stomach. But the day was pleasant. Songbirds trilled to one another across the forest canopy. The morning sun – warm, but not stifling – was like a balm to Burt's aching joints. He was almost merry as he blinked the last of the cobwebs from his eyes and began hiking upriver.

He didn't have long to travel. Only an hour or so from when he had set off, the low whine of car engines – rising and falling as they sped past in the distance – interrupted the chorus of birdsong and burbling water that had been his soundtrack to that point. Up ahead the river made a sharp turn. As he rounded the bend Burt saw a highway overpass spanning the water, connecting two sides of a narrow ravine the river had carved through the hills. Thanking his luck, he scrambled up the nearest hillside and hopped over the guardrail.

A sign not far from where he'd emerged told him he was standing on the side of Route 4. While it was hardly the busiest highway he could have hoped for, rarely a minute went by without a passing vehicle for him to wave down.

Getting one to stop, however, proved trickier. He was not the most attractive travelling companion, he knew. There are few things more off-putting than a person who is damp for unknown reasons. The spot he was standing in was also far from ideal, the berm narrow and on a bendy stretch of road with poor sightlines. Even if someone had wanted to stop, they wouldn't have chanced getting rear-ended. Burt turned and walked up the road a ways until it straightened out, stopping at last beside a gravel pull-off where the berm widened a bit.

The moment Burt saw the silver BMW in the distance he knew it was the car that would pick him up. There was no logical reason for his optimism. Twenty minutes had gone by since he'd changed spots, and dozens of vehicles had sped past without so much as acknowledging his existence. Nor was there anything about the make or color of the car that allowed him to intuit that the driver was the sort of person given to picking up hitchhikers in the middle of nowhere (if anything, the opposite was true).

Yet he was certain. It was something like a premonition, a series of events that unspooled like a montage in his mind, the way other people's memories did. Everything that transpired from that point – from the car's approach, to the little honk it gave as it pulled off the road, to the whir of the tinted window as it rolled down to reveal a middle-aged, goateed man behind the wheel, grinning at him with phosphorescent-white teeth – comported with Burt's visions. This in no way troubled or confused Burt. It was simply how things were.

The man told Burt to hop in, and they exchanged introductions. This was the first time Burt had tried out the name 'Burt Leathers' on another human being, and he was pleased to find that the driver – whose own name was Chuck – accepted it without question. Burt thanked Chuck for picking him up and apologized for his soggy clothes.

"Not at all," said Chuck. "A man should never apologize for being who he is. Besides, this baby's a rental." As they pulled out onto the road again, he reached over and twisted the volume knob on the radio. "You a Manilow head?"

Burt looked at him blankly.

"'Could It Be Magic'." Chuck pointed at the speakers, which were now emitting a plodding piano tune. "Barry Manilow?"

"Sorry, not familiar."

"The King," said Chuck, turning the volume up even further.

It did not take long for the conversation to turn to where Burt wanted to go. It was a topic he had dreaded since it had first occurred to him as being inevitable seconds earlier. Generally, one did not ask for a ride without a destination in mind, but Burt had been so preoccupied with getting out of the woods that he hadn't put any thought into the more difficult matter of where he wanted to get *to*.

"I think the nearest big town will do," he said.

"How big a big town?" said Chuck. "Raleigh big, or like, Tarboro big?"

"Either one."

"Well, what are you looking for? You need a phone?"

"A phone would be good."

"There's a gas station just up the road a bit. I could drop you there, they got a phone."

"That's ok. I can't remember who I need to call."

"You got any family around here?"

Burt shook his head.

"Where are you from?"

"Out of state."

"Which state?"

"This one."

"No, which state are you *from*?"

"Oh…I…Ohio?"

"You ain't sure?"

"I move around a lot."

"Must be quite a lot." Chuck took his eyes off the road for a moment to study his passenger's face. "What are you doing out here in the middle of nowhere?"

"Camping," said Burt.

"Camping? Shouldn't I take you back to your campsite?"

"No thanks."

"What about your stuff?"

"What stuff?"

"Your camping stuff!"

"Oh, that." Burt waved a hand. "I'm not worried about it."

"What about your car?"

"I came with someone else."

"What about them? You just going to leave them?"

Burt shrugged. He'd run out of creative dodges. "I just need to get to a big town," he said. "I lost my money, my license…everything." He took out his wallet and shook it in the air so Chuck could see how empty it was.

"Where'd you lose it?" said Chuck.

"Back there," said Burt. "In the woods."

"Don't you want to look for it?"

"I tried. No luck. My wallet was empty when I woke up this morning. I think I might have been robbed in my sleep."

Chuck frowned, but said nothing. They drove in silence for the next several miles.

There's something not quite right about this guy, thought Chuck, giving Burt another side-glance. Who in the world hadn't heard of Barry Manilow? It was unnerving. Not to mention all the other stuff. He was not a suspicious man by nature, but in his experience most people were able to tell you where they had come from, where they were going, and why. Maybe not in the broader, 'Why are any of us here?' sense, and maybe not amongst certain groups, like philosophy students or those with cognitive disorders, but still.

"You ever study philosophy?" said Chuck.

"No," said Burt, "why?"

"No reason." Chuck fidgeted in his seat. He had heard the same warnings everyone else had about the dangers of picking up hitchhikers, the possibility that one would turn out to be a criminal or deranged lunatic, but he had always dismissed them as paranoid propaganda. Now he began to speculate which type might be sitting next to him, staring straight ahead with pupils the size of buffalo nickels. "Say, maybe we ought to get you to a doctor."

"A doctor?" said Burt.

"You know, you wander out of the woods all wet, it sounds like you were out in the open overnight, you're disoriented. It might be a good idea to get checked out."

"That's all right. I feel fine."

"Ah." Chuck let the matter rest. He had noticed a strange feeling coming over him ever since he had stopped to pick up Burt. It had begun as a vibration, almost like a muscle spasm deep within his gut. Over time it had spread outward, first to the surface of the skin and then along his arms and legs, a tingling like when his blood sugar dropped too low. He had taken a swig from a bottle of soda he'd brought along, but the effect had not diminished; if anything, it had gotten worse. His breathing became labored, his forehead damp. More than anything, he felt light-headed, almost giddy, as if he'd been inhaling nitrous oxide.

He wanted to rest, to lie down somewhere, but first he had to get rid of his passenger. There was a town only a few miles away, Pebble Falls. It was a little hamlet, no more than two-thousand people, but Chuck reasoned that if Burt couldn't tell the difference between Raleigh and Tarboro, he wouldn't much object to Pebble Falls either.

They made it there in good time. Chuck drove down the main drag and finally pulled into an empty spot in front of the municipal building. True to his prediction, Burt simply thanked him for his help and clambered out onto the sidewalk.

As he drove away, waving goodbye in the rearview mirror, Chuck could already feel his body's equilibrium returning, the strange sensations beginning to fade. He couldn't explain what had caused them. He didn't blame Burt – who had done nothing but sit there, after all – but he was glad to see the back of him nonetheless. Still, a part of him wished he could stick around, if only to get some answers and see how the rest of this deeply strange man's story played out.

It played out like this – after Chuck had driven away, Burt walked into the municipal building and told the clerk he needed a new driver's license. The clerk asked him what had happened to his old license, and he told her he didn't know. "Lost?" she asked him. Burt didn't know. "Damaged?" she asked him. He didn't know. The clerk asked if he had two forms of identification. Only one, he told her, and pulled out his wallet to show her the name that was stitched inside.

"I think that's the company that made the wallet," said the clerk.

"It's possible," he conceded. "But it also happens to be my name."

"Burton Leathers?" she said.

"I usually go by Burt."

The clerk tried looking up his name in their systems, but there was no record of a Burt or Burton Leathers ever being issued a license by the State of North Carolina. Still, said Burt, there must be something she could do. She could issue him a state identification card, she told him, but she would need proof of residence and two forms of ID – a Social Security card and one other document establishing identity. And no, his wallet was not acceptable to establish identity.

Burt told the clerk he didn't have any of those things – they'd all been stolen. Did he have a police report, the clerk asked him? Not yet, he said. He would need to report the theft to the police first, she told him, then they would give him a report showing that his documents had been stolen.

Burt thanked the clerk and walked next door to the Pebble Falls police station. Twenty minutes later he returned and handed the clerk a sheet of pink carbon paper showing that his identity documents had been taken at an unknown time on an unknown date at an unspecified location.

Great, said the clerk, but unfortunately, she still wasn't able to help him. Now he would need to contact the Social Security Administration and provide them with a copy of the report in order to have his card reissued. Impossible, he told her, he didn't even know the Social Security Administration's phone number. I can help with that, said the clerk, and she disappeared into another room to find a phone book.

Anyone who has ever interacted with the bureaucratic state will find something familiar in the preceding interactions. They are hardly worth mentioning except for their notable outcome in this case, which is that an hour later Burt Leathers walked back out of the Pebble Falls municipal building with a duly-issued, laminated photo ID in his wallet. The winding road that led to this happy conclusion will not be recreated here, as the reader would find nothing illuminating in it. Suffice it to say that after tying one another in rhetorical knots for several minutes, the clerk simply came to the decision that issuing the card to Burt was the right thing to do.

Had she been confronted by her superiors and asked to defend her reasoning, she would have been hard-pressed to acquit herself. No regulation, policy, or procedural authority existed that was malleable enough to justify giving Burt Leathers a driver's license. She would have been left trying to convey the persuasiveness of the man himself – the last, pathetic refuge of the soon-to-be-condemned. Even there she would have found herself at a disadvantage, as the particulars of her conversation with Leathers had grown hazy and indistinct. The only thing she could remember in detail was a feeling in the room, a crackling energy as if the air itself were alive, like in the hours and minutes before a storm. This was not the sort of argument to sway the typical adjudicator, but as all this occurred in a one-horse town like Pebble Falls, in a time before the internet and automated background checks, no one much noticed or cared that a stranger had been issued a document in a name that might not be his. Life went on just the same.

In the following days, as he traveled from state to state, Burt would use his ID and police report to obtain a Social Security card, a passport, and even a replacement birth certificate. Each successive document became easier to acquire, to the point where he no longer had to rely on his strange persuasive powers anymore, but could simply provide the previous documents given to him as incontrovertible proof that he was who he was.

A bank in Tennessee processed his application for a checking account, and were so impressed by the interaction that they ended up offering him a job as a sales representative. He worked there for a time, earning Employee of the Month honors at two separate branches, but soon felt constricted and decided to move on. From there – as detailed in his biography, *Finding My Way*, a complimentary gift provided to all True North Platinum Plus members – he spent time at a car dealership in Texarkana, an insurance company in Dodge City, and a jeweler in Colorado Springs, achieving distinction in each instance but soon growing restless, convinced that the universe had bigger plans in mind for him.

It wasn't until a stint at an outdoor-gear rental shop in Jackson Hole, Wyoming – where an entire display case worth of compasses pointed toward him wherever he went – that Leathers hit upon those plans. "They must know that you're our North Star," said a new hire, whom Leathers had been tasked with training on the register.

"It was this confluence of events – my growing confidence, a strange phenomenon, a chance remark – that set the stage for my rise to power," Leathers wrote. But that's another book for another time.

Eight

Leathers sat in the makeshift office he had fashioned for himself in a utility closet down the hall from the executive suite, mulling over a crossword puzzle. In the corner opposite him, his chief counsel, Stilton Farnsworth, waited patiently, perched atop an overturned mop bucket.

"Stilt," said Leathers. "What's a 16-letter word meaning 'sleight of hand'?"

"Prestidigitation," said Stilton.

Leathers furrowed his brow, then looked down at the puzzle again. "Starts with an *m*," he said.

"How's that?"

"I've got *Manilow* going the other way."

"What's the clue?"

"*The King, in rock and roll parlance.*"

"That's *Presley*," said Stilton.

"Elvis Presley?"

Stilton nodded.

"Hmm..." After some hesitation, Leathers flipped his pencil around and busied himself with the eraser.

Leathers' real office had been turned over to Salvatore Slocum, the new Interim CEO of True North, LLC, who had just been named to the position a few hours earlier in a hastily put-together ceremony in the company cafeteria. The announcement had been met with the sort of bemused murmuring that accompanies shocking news about a subject toward which people are generally indifferent. Only those for whom True North, LLC was a significant part of their identity felt anything like ill will toward Sal; Sheila was particularly upset at the injustice of it all. Amongst the others, the prevailing sentiment was that of confusion mixed with a profound desire to know whether snacks would be provided.

The hasty distribution of surplus pudding cups placated the latter group, and as for the former there was little recourse but to stamp their feet or mutter to an office full of largely unsympathetic ears. "I'm rather pleased with how that came off," said Leathers, once his crossword had been amended.

Stilton nodded. "Not nearly the pushback we had expected. I thought I was in for a long day, but aside from that one question about refreshments everyone just seemed to accept the fact that Sal's the boss now."

Leathers grunted, but said nothing. He had noticed that as well. It was the only thing that dampened his pleasure at how smoothly his plan had gone. He and Stilton had spent the previous evening workshopping an intricate explanation for why Leathers needed to step aside temporarily, and why Sal was the right man to fill the position. They had even prepared draft responses to any potential questions they might receive. In the end, none of it had been needed. It wasn't the wasted time that bothered Leathers so much as learning that his workforce saw him as replaceable. Better to suffer a hard truth than a bullet to the head, he reasoned, but that didn't mean his pride was any less wounded.

"Burt," said Stilton, "I was wondering if I could ask you a favor. It's about my court case."

"Ah, yes, the case," said Leathers, happy for the change of subject. "How's that going?"

"Not bad," said Stilton. "That First Circuit decision was a real setback. Still, I submitted my appeal to the State Supreme Court yesterday, and an old law school buddy of mine who clerks over there tells me the justices are likely to take it up."

"Good, good."

"I was hoping I could take an extended leave of absence to work on my argument. My brief was a little rushed, and I want to make sure everything is airtight before we go to trial. Nothing crazy, mind you, just a month or two."

"A month or two?" Leathers gnawed at his pencil. "Gee Stilt, I don't know. You know I'd do anything for you, but this is a pretty dicey time to be without my chief counsel. What happens if this lunatic who's been threatening me never shows up? What if he does show and botches things? I want to make sure

I'm getting my job back if Slocum survives, you know what I mean?"

"Don't worry," said Stilton. "I drafted the paperwork myself. You maintain complete control throughout Sal's tenure. The contract can be terminated at any point with just your signature."

"What if he finds a loophole to exploit? Or a clause?" Leathers frowned. "Which one is it people exploit, loopholes or clauses?"

"Neither, in this case. I had the team go over everything with a fine-tooth comb. It's rock solid." Stilton shrugged. "Besides, I don't think he even wants to be CEO."

"That's what I had thought. It's one of the main reasons I chose him for this. But now…" Leathers sighed and shifted his gaze to the center of the room, thinking back on his meeting with Sal the day before. "I was getting worried that maybe he was *too* indolent to make a convincing CEO, that the shooter wouldn't buy it. I decided to take him under my wing, teach him a little about what it means to be a leader. I figured I'd kill two birds with one stone, provide an orientation to help sell him on the idea that this handover is the real deal, and at the same time make sure he knows how to walk and talk and act like a boss."

"Did it work?"

"Too well. I don't know what I unlocked in that kid, but it was plain as day he was relishing being in charge. You know me, Stilt, I can read people. I'm telling you this guy's got me worried."

"He shouldn't. Like I said, one swipe of the pen and he's right back to being a sales rep."

"Maybe you're right." Leathers remembered how his meeting with Sal had ended, how nervous the younger man had been when it was just the two of them together, trembling and dripping sweat. It was clear he understood who the real authority figure was. He pushed it out of his mind. "Anyway, this case of yours, is it likely to get much publicity?"

"Plenty," said Stilton. "The *Ashburg Chronicler* called it 'the most egregiously frivolous lawsuit since the McDonald's hot coffee affair'."

"I remember that one."

"My law school buddy says the justices believe my case *presents a novel question of contract law as it applies to higher education*." Stilton made air quotes around this last part. "There's even a chance the federal Supreme Court could take it up down the road, given the national implications."

"The big leagues, huh?" Leathers thought for a moment. "Doesn't this make me look kind of ridiculous, though? I mean, there you are arguing that you're a garbage attorney with a shit education, and I'm the guy who hired you to be my chief counsel."

"Not at all. In fact, I go to great lengths to attribute whatever legal acumen I possess to your benevolence and tutelage."

Leathers scoffed. "Tell you what – I'll give you the two months off on the following conditions. First, you agree to work a minimum of five references to True North, LLC or the True North motivational system into your oral arguments. Second, if anything goes wrong with the plan here, you drop whatever you're doing and hustle back to take care of it."

"Done!" Stilton leapt from his seat to grasp Leathers' hand. "Thank you, Burt! You don't know how much this means to me."

"Come now," said Leathers.

"No, I mean it. If there's anything pressing you need me to take care of before my leave starts, just say the word."

"Nothing at all. Just keep your phone close in case things go south."

"I promise. And don't worry, everything will be fine." Stilton smiled and clapped Leathers on the shoulder before scurrying from the office.

A strained smile, Leathers noted. Stilton was as close to a friend as Leathers had at True North, yet even he seemed to grow uncomfortable when he spent too much time in Leathers' presence. *Am I really so much of a tyrant?* Leathers wondered. If anything, he felt he was rather lax as a boss. Yes, he demanded commitment and a certain level of professionalism from his employees, but what CEO didn't? Wasn't he always smiling at people in the halls? Didn't he encourage morale-building events? Hadn't Hawaiian Shirt Day been his idea?

Even Sunny, with whom he'd had several brief flings over the years, kept a respectful distance most of the time. The first time they'd had sex, in his office, she had staggered back to her desk afterwards as if she were drunk. He'd been flattered, chalking it up to post-coital exhaustion, but enough had happened over the intervening years that he could no longer maintain that delusion. It was a conundrum – all the wisdom and insightfulness he had gained after achieving enlightenment, and yet there were these glaring blind spots when it came to understanding himself. He stared at the door, wondering what Stilton was thinking at that very moment.

****

As the door closed behind him, Stilton rifled through his pockets looking for his cell phone. The dizziness and tightness in his chest were already receding. He had long ago stopped trying to explain why being close to Leathers brought on these symptoms. It was just something one had to deal with, like bundling up against the cold whenever winter came around. Instead, he focused on mitigation, keeping just enough distance between them that the sensations never became overwhelming. That was proving harder with the new office setup. The quarters were so cramped that it was impossible to maintain any meaningful separation. Yet another reason this extended leave was such a blessing. Hopefully by the time he got back this whole affair would be behind them, and Leathers would be ensconced in the executive suite once again.

He found the phone and picked out a secluded spot near the fire exit to call Grace. His first attempt went to voicemail, as did his second, but the third proved to be the proverbial charm. After the first ring there was a click, and a woman's voice snapped, "*What is it?*" through the receiver.

"Incredible news," he said. "You won't believe it. I just got done talking to Burt, and…"

"Not now," she cut him off.

"But darling…"

"I'm busy."

"Grace, please…"

"*Graciela.*"

"You're not going to get me to argue with you, I'm in too good a mood. Listen, I just had a meeting with Burt, and he…"

"Stilty, don't you know what day it is?"

Stilton frowned and craned his neck to look at the clock on the wall, before remembering that clocks only tell time. "Wednesday? Is that right? I know it's a quarter past one."

"Do you remember the project we discussed?"

"The feminist void thing?"

"My *instructional method*, yes. It just so happens that I'm in the middle of a guiding session as we speak."

"Is that what you call your classes?"

Stilton could feel Grace bristle through the phone. "*Yes*," she said.

"I didn't know you'd started with those already."

"That's because I didn't tell you."

"In that case it hardly seems fair to get mad at me for not knowing what day it is."

"You're right, Stilty, how clumsy of me. I take it all back, let's talk more tonight over dinner and you can tell me your big news. We'll have lemon chicken, ta!" She hung up the phone before Stilton could respond, then put the ringer on mute.

"Now," she said, turning to the man in the green turtleneck standing beside her, who had introduced himself as Skip. "Look around you. I want you to write what you see."

Skip adjusted his glasses, which had been steadily working their way down his nose. Fifteen minutes earlier he had intercepted a flyer tumbling down the sidewalk and returned it to an elegant yet frazzled woman who was careering after it in platform heels. Now he found himself standing in the middle of a median strip in downtown Ashburg, next to that same woman, being instructed in the art of 'radical observation'.

"Just to be clear, this isn't costing me money, is it?" said Skip.

"This is your free introductory session, as we discussed," said Grace. "Though donations are always welcome." She swept her arm in front of her, like an empress indicating her dominion. "Now, write! Exactly as you see it!"

Skip blinked his eyes at her, then turned and surveyed the bustling street scene with the expression of a manatee taking in a performance of *Pagliacci*. Several moments passed this way, to the point where Grace began to worry he had suffered a catatonic episode. She decided to remain quiet and let the artistic process take its course, and was rewarded when Skip suddenly hunched over the notepad and began scribbling furiously. When at last his pencil stopped moving, Grace asked to see what he'd written.

"The man walked down the street," she read, "wearing a brown suit and carrying a briefcase. He had a hurried, agitated gait. Every so often he would glance at his watch. When he reached the corner he waited for the traffic signal, then dashed across Fourth Avenue toward the marina…"

"Well?" said Skip, when she had finished.

Grace shrugged. "It's fine."

"What's wrong with it?" said Skip.

"Nothing. It's ok."

"You said I should write what I see."

"I did."

"Well?"

"It's just…well, like here."

"Where?"

Grace pointed.

"Every so often he would glance at his watch," read Skip. He looked up. "That's what he did."

"Yes, but why?" said Grace.

"To see what time it was, I suppose."

"That's supposition."

"I can't very well observe why he's looking at his watch."

"You don't know what you're capable of." She grabbed him by the shoulders and pulled him closer. Their eyes locked. "Look harder. Look *deeper*. I want you to interrogate the how and the why of the everyday, to navigate past the performative markers of *self* and find the liminal truth that exists between our environmental constructs and organic composition."

"Oh," said Skip. He freed himself from her grasp and turned back toward the street. All he saw were people on their lunch break. A woman in a tan peacoat was hurrying down the sidewalk, obviously late for something. She barely broke stride as she raised her arm and pulled back her sleeve to check what time it was. *No,* he thought, *no more watches.* The door to a deli swung open, and a man emerged carrying a sandwich wrapped in wax paper. Something made him turn back, and he caught the door before it closed and held it for an elderly woman who was on her way in. *What was the lesson here?* Skip wondered. *Something about the obligations imposed on us from above versus the obligation to our fellow humans? Compassion as a coping mechanism for this alien world in which we've entrapped ourselves?* Mostly, his thoughts returned to the sandwich. An angry rumbling in his stomach demanded attention. He checked his own watch and gasped.

"I really need to get back to work," he said to Grace. "I haven't even eaten yet today."

"Use that hunger," she said. "Let it awaken your senses. Here…" She scanned the sidewalk, then put her hand on Skip's shoulder and pointed. "Those two, tell me about them. Describe what you *see.*"

Skip looked where Grace was indicating and spotted a couple – a man and woman – walking arm in arm. Even if Grace had not singled them out, Skip couldn't have missed them. The man was shaped like a traffic cone and wore a western shirt with a string tie.

On top of his head perched a Stetson hat so wide it cleared the sidewalk in front of them like a cowcatcher, providing ample shade for both him and the voluptuous woman clinging to his side. (*'Voluptuous' or 'Rubenesque'*, he considered? She seemed to fall somewhere in the middle. Perhaps this was one of those liminal truths he was supposed to be discovering.) They sauntered along at a pace completely at odds with everyone around them, leaning in close to murmur to one another as if sharing a secret.

"Something's not right," he said to Grace.

"How do you mean?" she said.

"With those two. I can't put my finger on it."

"Try."

Skip looked at the couple again and frowned. "It's not anything they're doing. More of a feeling, really."

Grace knew just what he meant. She had felt it too. A vague sense of menace seemed to radiate from them, like cold from a block of ice. "Describe it for me."

"I can't. I told you, it doesn't make any sense."

"It doesn't have to *make sense*," she said, making air quotes. "If everything true also made sense we wouldn't need psychiatrists. We wouldn't need art."

"I suppose."

"Just say the first thing that comes into your head."

"There's nothing…"

"Say it! The very first word!"

"Murder!" said Skip. His eyes went wide, and he turned sheepishly toward Grace. "Or vengeance. I thought of both at the same time. Does that make sense?"

No, thought Grace, looking back across the street, *but it does sound true.*

Nine

Sal examined the phone/intercom system on his desk, poring over its cluttered display with the concentration of a scholar deciphering one of the Dead Sea Scrolls. Its system of abbreviations and symbols was no less inscrutable to him. More than once he had summoned the courage to lift the receiver from its cradle and press a random button, only to be rewarded with some combination of electronic bleating, flashing lights, and an alarming digital message ("Er 9303; VoIP No EX 5.86 NULL!", for example) scrolling across its screen. It was frustrating enough that he was almost thankful to see Sunny's shadow creeping beneath his door every couple of minutes as she attempted to eavesdrop from the hallway.

"Sunny, can you come in here for a moment please?" he shouted.

The shadow jumped, as much as such a thing is possible, then abruptly vanished. A few seconds later there was a knock at the door, followed by Sunny poking her head inside. "Did you call for me, sir?"

"Yes, please come in."

"I thought I heard someone yelling my name," she said, grinning pleasantly, if a cat's amusement at watching a gutted mouse writhing on the ground could be called 'pleasant'. "Mr. Leathers usually rang me on the intercom when he needed something." She shrugged. "If that's something you'd like to try."

"Excellent suggestion," said Sal, through gritted teeth. He gestured to the phone. "Would you mind giving me a quick walkthrough?"

"Not at all!" Sunny glided around behind the desk, bringing with her the scent of peony and lilac. She had made her displeasure with Sal's elevation known from the moment it had been announced, greeting the news with a pout that – when paired with her voluminous blonde hair – made her look like a Brigitte Bardot impersonator. Since then, she had spent most of her time making caustic remarks and looking for ways to sully Sal's reputation on the floor, which would also serve – she hoped – to create a groundswell of nostalgia for her dear, departed Mr. Leathers.

"Just press this button here," she said, drawing out each word, the way one speaks when explaining something to a toddler. "That will connect you to our intercom system. Press here to turn on the speaker…" She pressed a button, and the sound of a dial tone filled the room. "Then enter the three-digit number of the person you want to speak to."

"What's your number?" said Sal.

"Why, 301. Don't you have a copy of the directory?"

"I guess not."

"I'm surprised Mr. Leathers didn't go over all of this with you before he left."

"It all happened so quickly. It probably just slipped his mind."

"Of *course*." She tilted her head and sighed, as if he were a puppy who'd gotten tangled in its own leash. "If you need me to show you how to do anything else, I'm just a few button-presses away."

"301," said Sal.

"Very good!"

Sal practiced his deep breathing as the door swung closed, inhaling the last traces of Sunny's perfume. A few minutes ago he hadn't known how to use the phone, he reminded himself, and now he did. That was worth whatever condescension he had to put up with. Still, her comment about Leathers stuck with him, mainly because he had been wondering the same thing. Why hadn't Leathers shown him these things? Yes, he had given Sal a few lessons in 'being a leader', but what about the phone? What about the computer? What were half of these files he had come across while browsing through the shared drive? Where was his calendar? What upcoming meetings did he have? It was almost as if Leathers had no interest in making sure he knew how to run the company, only that he looked the part.

Sal felt adrift. He needed someone to talk to. He pressed the intercom button, then the speaker button, then dialed '3-0-1'.

"Practice run?" said Sunny.

Sal took another deep breath. "No, business call. Can you please tell Colleen Frink to come to my office?"

"Of course. May I tell her the reason?"

"I'll tell her when she gets here, thank you."

"Shall I tell her to come immediately?"

"Please."

Sal hung up and waited. A few minutes later there was a knock on the door, and Sunny poked her head inside. "I have Colleen Frink here to see you?"

"Yes, Sunny. Thank you. Please send her in."

Before Sunny could step aside, Colleen shouldered her out of the way and closed the door in her face. Sal had never seen her look so serious as she strode across the room and planted herself in the chair across from him.

"We need to talk," she said.

Sal held up a finger for her to be quiet, then pointed to the far side of the room, where Sunny's shadow could be seen slithering across the carpet through the gap under the door. He reached for the phone and dialed '3-0-1' again. The shadow abruptly vanished.

"She never stops," he said, hanging up. "It's like working for the Stasi."

"I know why you asked me here," said Colleen.

Sal blinked at her. "You do?"

"Yes. And let me just say upfront that I find it wholly inappropriate. There's no room in the workplace for physical relationships, let alone one between a manager and his subordinate. That's not to say I'm not flattered, as a woman, to be desired physically, but my morals will not allow me to enter into a tryst on company property. It would be a betrayal of myself, my coworkers, my…"

"I didn't ask you here to have sex," said Sal.

"You didn't?"

"No, what made you think that?"

"Isn't that why bosses ask female employees to come to their offices?"

"You need to stop watching *48 Hours*, Colleen, it's rotting your brain." Sal shook his head. "I just needed someone to talk to."

"Oh, well…in that case, if you could only eat one food for the rest of your life what would it be?" She grimaced. "Sorry, that's kind of basic, I know."

"Salad," said Sal.

"Why salad?"

"Because you can put anything you want on a salad."

"Hmm…" Colleen's eyes narrowed. "That's true. Feels kind of cheap, but I suppose I never stipulated that you could only have one type of salad. I guess I'll have to allow it." She nodded. "Very shrewd. I can see now why they decided to put you in charge."

"I can't," Sal moped. "That's what I wanted to talk to you about. I have no idea what I'm supposed to be doing."

"Didn't Mr. Leathers tell you anything before he left?"

"Only that I should always appear confident and pretend like I know what I'm doing. He said I shouldn't be afraid to make decisions and stick by them, no matter what. But I don't even know how to find a decision to make. Mostly I just sit here and wait for something to happen."

"Is that so bad? They pay you either way, right? If it makes you feel better, I never got the impression Mr. Leathers did much during the day either."

"I'd like to do *something.* I feel like a fraud."

Colleen nodded. "That's the difference between us and them. You're not management, not in your heart. You're just a worker, like me. You believe, deep down, that money is something that needs to be earned, when really it's something to be accumulated. Until you make that switch up here," she pointed to her head, "you'll never be one of them. No one gets rich because they *earned* it."

"I don't care about getting rich. I just want to be useful."

"If that's the case, why not fix all the problems around here?"

"What problems?"

"*What problems?*" repeated Colleen. "How about all the stuff we're always complaining about on the floor – the terrible pay, the awful leave policy, the stupid scripts we have to follow…there are so many things you could change."

"How would I do that?"

"You're in charge, right? Write a memo. Send it to all the department heads. You decide what to do, it's up to everyone else to figure out *how* to do it."

A smile spread across Sal's face. "That's not bad. Care to help?"

"Sure. There must be a memo template and an org chart somewhere on this computer." Colleen grinned like a jack-o-lantern as she pulled her chair around to the other side of the desk. "Let's make all our dreams come true!"

****

The sound of high heels clicking across the linoleum could be heard in the distance, starting out faint but growing steadily louder. Leathers put a hand to his chest, feeling it vibrate like a double-bass drum. His heartrate accelerated, beating in rhythm with the 'tick-tick-tick' sound approaching from down the hall. He knew it was Sunny on the march long before she burst into his office.

"It's terrible!" she cried. In her hand was a piece of paper, which she waved back and forth as if swatting at invisible horseflies. "He's lost his mind!"

"Dammit Sunny, shut the door!" hissed Leathers. "What good is a secret office if everyone knows about it?"

Sunny pulled herself together long enough to comply. Once the door was closed, she scurried across the room and slapped the paper on his desk. "Look at this! Look at what he's doing!"

Leathers eyed her dubiously, then produced a pair of reading glasses from his pocket and began skimming the page. By the time he reached the bottom his face had contorted like a mime's acting out a cerebral embolism.

"He didn't!" Leathers sputtered. "A twenty-percent raise across the board? Four weeks of vacation and unlimited paid sick leave? A free, all-you-can-eat nacho bar?"

Sunny nodded to indicate that Sal, in fact, had done all of those things.

"This went out to the entire senior team," said Leathers. "It's already in motion. He's going to bankrupt the company!"

"You can stop him, right?" said Sunny.

"I don't know." Short of voiding Sal's contract and reestablishing control – which would put him right back in the same predicament he was in before – he wasn't sure there was anything he could do.

He cursed himself for letting Stilton leave. He would have to call up his chief counsel, get an idea of what his options were. At least he still had Sunny, he thought. She was far from discreet – he had hesitated for a good long time before deciding to let her in on his plan – but she was loyal and cunning and looked terrific in a golf dress. He thought about those early days, slipping out in the afternoon to hit the links, late-night assignations on the 18th green. Those were happier times. Perhaps it was time to rekindle the flame, he thought. He found himself growing sentimental, weepy. Old age had him in its grip.

"You did well," he said. "I'm going to need you to keep a close eye on things from here on out. Every move he makes, every person who visits his office, every overheard scrap of conversation, I want you to report it back to me, understand?"

Sunny shook her head. "I can't. I'm no longer his administrative assistant!"

Leathers gasped. "He fired you?"

"Reclassified," she pouted. "I'm an Operations Support Specialist, whatever that means."

"A demotion?"

"No, the salary is the same. Actually, I'll be making twenty percent more once the raise goes through. But I'm all the way on the other side of the building now. By the *mailroom*."

"My God." For the first time since hatching his plot, Leathers began to wonder whether he had outfoxed himself. So much time and planning had gone into ensuring he was nowhere near the executive's chair when that madman who'd been threatening to kill him finally appeared, and just as much into figuring out how to reinstall himself once danger had been averted. He had barely considered what might happen in the interim, the damage that could be done in such a short time by any yutz who got it into his head that he was Che Guevara reborn and could right the world's wrongs by doling out the company's money like candy from a parade float. What was it that had made him trust Slocum so easily? There was a natural inclination there, a fondness he rarely felt for anyone, let alone someone who was a relative stranger. He had grown soft, started believing in his intuition too much.

"We need to tighten things up," he said. "Do what we can to mitigate the damage."

The beginnings of a smile flickered across Sunny's face. She loved when he spoke decisively. "What do you have in mind?"

"You know that electronics store near the courthouse?"

Sunny shook her head.

"Never mind, I'll write down the address. I want you to pay a visit when you leave here tonight. If we can't have you snooping around his office anymore, then we'll have to find a less conspicuous way to keep tabs on what's happening in there."

Ten

The guard's eyes goggled at the woman shimmying toward him up the steps, all double-wide curves and too-bronze skin, as if some ancient fertility goddess had been reborn as a waitress at a Florida Waffle House.

Little happened in the lobby of 17 Industry Way, Building C that was novel. Even the faces that passed through – stopping briefly to hand over their ID cards for a cursory scan and a few seconds of banter about sports or the weather or whatever bit of small talk had formed the beginning, and now the entirety, of their relationship – rarely changed, to the point where they became just another part of the décor, like the ferns or marble columns. There was no mistaking this woman for a fern. A vision of eros in business casual, she sashayed over and pressed herself against the desk, parting her lips enigmatically. The guard squeaked.

That was just the reaction Elmie had been banking on when, that morning, she had squeezed into a stretch top and pencil skirt one size too small and plastered on her favorite red lipstick. This was not the time for subtlety. She had worked in enough places with enough security guards to know that the idle mind tended toward daydream, and the daydreamer toward ostentatious fantasy. Men were not difficult creatures to gauge, least of all a man who had spent years behind a desk watching life go by. The moment she saw the salt and pepper in the guard's mustache, she knew he was hers.

"Well…" he said, pausing to drink her in. "What can I do you for?"

Ugh, thought Elmie. "Be my knight in shining armor, I'm hoping."

"Oh," he chuckled. His hand involuntarily went to the badge on his shirt, making sure it was straight. "I'll do my best."

"I seem to have got myself into quite a pickle." Elmie did her best Shirley Temple pout. "I dragged myself halfway across the country for a conference here at True North – I work out at their distribution center in Almandine, you see. You ever been to Almandine?"

"Can't say I'm familiar."

"Beautiful place. You ever make it out that way I'll show you around. You can have a lot of fun in Almandine if you know the right people."

"I'm gonna hold you to that," said the guard, already tabulating how much vacation time he had saved up.

"You better," she giggled. "Here's the thing. No sooner do I get settled into my hotel room than I remember my ID card expired last week." As she said this, she sent two fingers plunging down beneath her neckline – dragging the guard's gaze along with them – to retrieve the card in question. He accepted it from her as if it were a holy relic.

"I called my bosses back in Almandine to ask them what I should do, and they told me building security…that's you…" Elmie winked "…can temporarily reactivate it for me until the conference is over." *Time for the coup de grace*, she thought, and in one fluid motion flipped her hair, shifted her weight to accentuate her curves and ever so slightly turned up the corners of her mouth in a flirtatious smile. "So, what do you say? Are you my white knight?"

The guard was already at his computer, in the process of inserting Elmie's ID into the card reader, before the dopey smile left his face, replaced by a look of consternation. "You say it's a conference you're in town for?"

"That's right," said Elmie. "Nothing big, just a couple days with some of the operations staff from around the country. You know, shipping, logistics, all that fun stuff." She added a ditzy eyeroll.

"The companies usually notify us in advance if they're going to be having any sort of event going on."

"Like I said, it's pretty small. Just a handful of people. They probably didn't think it was worth mentioning."

Elmie had a sinking feeling in her stomach. If there was one other thing she knew about men who spent their entire lives behind the same desks, it's that they weren't the type to play fast and loose with the rules. She could see her plan starting to unravel. On a whim, she raised herself up on her tiptoes and leaned down low over the counter. "I *really* hope this won't be an issue."

The guard looked as though someone were tearing his heart from his chest. "I'm really, really sorry for the inconvenience, Ms. Duncan," he said, very much not looking her in the eyes. "I just need to call up to True North and verify that there's a conference this week." He held up his hands. "*Not* that I don't believe you, of course. It's just standard procedure we have to follow."

Elmie could see he was even more nervous than she was. No doubt he saw whatever chance he thought he might have had with her slipping away. Nothing cooled off a woman like deferring to standard procedure.

"Do you have to?" she said. "I'd hate to give them a bad first impression. You know, showing up with an ID that doesn't even work."

"Now who could have a bad impression of you?" he said, trying to rekindle the flame. A tepid smile was the best Elmie could manage. "Don't worry," he said, "I promise we'll have everything squared away in a minute."

Elmie watched with increasing desperation as the guard laid her card on the desk and picked up the phone. She had not been so vain as to think there was no way her plan could fail, but until that moment she had not appreciated the difficulties of extracting herself if things started going wrong. What would happen when the guard spoke to the people at True North and learned there was no conference? Could she play it off as a misunderstanding? Would they let her walk away without questioning?

"Hey there," said the guard into the phone, interrupting her thoughts. "This is security down at the front desk. There's a woman here who says she's in town for an operations conference you all are supposed to be having this week, but we don't seem to have any record of it."

I could leave right now, thought Elmie. They had no reason, no right to hold her. But the guard had her ID. They knew who she was. If she took off running it would look suspicious. Would they pursue charges, accuse her of trespassing, misrepresentation?

"Uh huh," said the guard. "Come up from Almandine, she said. *Almandine.* Her ID's having issues, so I was going to reset it for her..."

Maybe that was all the more reason to disappear, she thought. Surely the cops had better things to do than launch a multistate manhunt for someone who showed up to an office building with an expired ID. How could they prove she'd committed a crime? More than likely they'd take a statement, let the company confiscate the card and leave it at that. But if she was right here, able to answer questions, they might decide to press her a little. Once she started talking who knew what she might let slip? And if she refused to talk, things might go even worse.

"Ok," said the guard. "Ok. Ok, I'll tell her. Thanks."

As the guard took the receiver from his ear, there was a final, fleeting moment where a voice in Elmie's head screamed at her to run. Her legs trembled, as if even her muscles were at war over what to do. But in the end, inertia won out. She stared at him as he hung up the phone, too anxious to remember to bat her eyelashes or arch her back.

"All cleared up," he said with a smile.

"What's that?" she managed to croak.

"I told you it wouldn't take but a minute." He grabbed the ID off the desk and popped it into the card reader, then started typing. "I can get you general building access right now that covers the outer doors and the stairwells and what have you. Once you get up on the fourth floor, the True North people can give you additional access to whichever offices or conference rooms you'll need."

A few clicks of the mouse, and the guard removed the card and handed it back to Elmie. "You're all set, pretty lady." Now that he had come through for her in her time of need his confidence was on the rise again. "Maybe once you're finished upstairs we could get together and make plans for that tour of Almandine you promised me."

"I'd like that," she said, swooning as if she were drunk. Her cheeks flushed red, which seemed to embarrass the guard even more than showing off her boobs had. He lowered his eyes like a bashful child. "Fourth floor," he said, pointing toward a bank of elevators along the back wall.

"Thank you," said Elmie, turning to go. "You've been very sweet."

She scurried away while her luck still held. Halfway across the lobby she glanced over her shoulder and saw the guard was still watching her. He grinned broadly and waved. Elmie waved back without turning, hoping it looked coquettish, and hurried over to join the group of people clustered around the elevator doors.

Off to her right, past the elevators, was a hallway branching off from the main lobby. Elmie worked her way around the edge of the group until she could peer down its length. When she squinted, she could make out some windows at the far end, and through them what looked like a statue of a Croatian sniper in the plaza outside. *That must be the place,* she thought.

From the corner of her eye, she could see the guard at the front desk speaking to someone. She waited until he turned his back, then slipped away from the group and hurried down the hall and through the door at the end marked 'Stairwell B'. Past the foot of the stairs was an exit door; Elmie pressed the crossbar and popped it open, then stuck her head outside.

Bagley waited a few feet away, leaning against the side of the building. He looked like a musician on a smoke break between sets at the Grand Ole Opry. His hands were buried in the pockets of his Nudie suit jacket. One foot was propped up against the wall, showing off the contours of his caiman leather boots. A cigarette dangled from his mouth, barely visible beneath the brim of his Stetson, which he wore low as if tucking in for a siesta.

"Daggum," he said, when he saw who it was. Smoke seeped out from between his lips as he spoke. "I might've known you'd pull it off, but that don't mean I'm one bit less impressed. You surely are some master of the dark arts."

"Can you be a little more discreet?" said Elmie. "How many singing cowboys you see around here?"

"I ain't singing anything."

"At least take off that stupid hat. You're going to get us both pinched."

"I think the time for stealth has reached its conclusion." He dropped his cigarette and ground it into the pavement with his heel. "It's high noon."

"It's ten-thirty," said Elmie.

"Metaphorically speaking." Bagley adopted a gunfighter's stance. "What do you think? Do I remind you of Gary Cooper?"

"Aside from the fame, looks, and money I'd say you're a dead ringer."

"What are you so snippy about? Relax! We're in, ain't we?"

"Not yet," she said, grabbing him by the sleeve. "Come on, before the alarm goes off."

"Lead the way, darling." He followed her inside, the Colt revolver stashed beneath his jacket slapping lightly against his ribs with every step. Maybe this scheme of his was more Frank Miller than Marshal Kane, he considered. Either way, it made for one hell of a movie.

****

Colleen poked her head into the office. Sal had been cloistered there since early that morning interviewing employees off the floor. One idea he had seized upon since becoming CEO was that everyone at

162

True North, from the lowliest clerk to the highest executive, had latent talents that were not being properly nurtured and cultivated by the company. Workers needed to be stimulated, he believed, given an outlet to take the things they were passionate about in life and apply them to the True North mission, thereby finding fulfillment at the same time they were helping to increase the company's bottom line.

Whether this was an original insight or insomnia-induced drivel that not even the dullest venture capitalist could get excited about was debatable; certainly, Sal had not been sleeping any better of late. His sunken eyes and gaping mouth were like the finger holes on a bowling ball. Colleen imagined herself on league night at the Lucky Strike, flinging his head down the lane to pick up a seven-ten split.

"It's an Illuminati pyramid," said Doug Sheets.

"I see that." Sal stared at the crudely sketched triangle with an eyeball at the top on Doug's bare chest. "Why are you showing it to me?"

"You asked what I care about, who I am. This sums it up better than any explanation I could give you."

"You might be right." Sal leaned forward and squinted, which in his current condition seemed to suck his eyeballs out of their sockets straight through to the back of his skull. "Is that writing at the bottom?"

"'Living life one day at a time'," read Doug, running his finger along the words. He shrugged. "That's just how I feel about things."

"I see."

"This total smokeshow I met at a house party in Watertown did it for me." He began buttoning up his shirt. "She told me she was working on getting her tattoo license, so I let her practice on me. One-hundred percent free."

"Skin's looking a bit angry there."

"Yeah, it hurts like balls."

"All that red there around the edges."

"I know. Feels like a bad sunburn. You think maybe it's infected?"

Sal held out his hands. "If you worry about things like that, are you really living one day at a time?"

Doug nodded. "You're right. Thanks for keeping me honest." He grasped Sal's hand and shook it, then winked at Colleen on his way out the door.

"So, what's Doug's hidden talent?" she said, stepping into the room.

"Honestly, I forgot that's why I called him in here in the first place."

"You ok?"

Sal nodded.

"You look terrible."

Sal nodded.

"Didn't you say you were going to go to bed extra early?"

"I meant to, but then I stayed up all night writing a letter to the city about how I can't sleep."

"Listen, security is on the phone. Do you know anything about an operations conference? One of the attendees is downstairs, says she needs building access."

"Nothing," said Sal. He shuffled some things around on his desk, then lifted his stapler, not knowing what he was looking for. "That's hardly a surprise, I guess. You know anything about operations?"

"Nothing. What should we do?"

"Tell them to send her up. We'll toss her in one of the conference rooms until we figure out what to do with her. Maybe if we put everyone who shows up in there together, they'll all start talking and the conference will take care of itself."

"Will do."

"Oh, and can you find out who arranged for this?" He pointed at the potted plant on the table behind him. A card taped to the front, 'Congratulations and welcome to our new CEO!', and was signed, 'Your True North, LLC Family'. "I want to send them a thank-you note, let them know how much I appreciate it."

****

"Who is that who just came in?" said Leathers.

"Colleen," said Sunny.

"Who's that?"

"That stork he replaced me with."

"That what?"

"That's what she looks like with those knobby stick legs."

"Now…"

"She looks like a stork. She looks like Big Bird!"

"Big Bird was a canary."

"I'm way prettier than she is."

"Looks aren't everything, Sun Bun." Leathers blinked, then grimaced. He could hear his eyelids as they closed and opened. They made a sound like someone dragging a box across a concrete floor.

Sal was not the only one who had been up all night. Leathers, for his part, had not even left the building. Until the wee hours of the morning he had been in his old office working to install the surveillance equipment Sunny had picked up earlier that evening.

"How could you send me to a place like that?" she had said upon returning from her shopping trip. "That was not an electronics store."

"What's all this stuff, then?" said Leathers. He gestured to the floor of his office, where Sunny had dumped several bags worth of electronic components – cameras, microphones, routers, adapters, circuits, sensors, plus an old Elbex CCTV monitor whose screen broadcast images in a murky, spectral green. Wires twisted and coiled their way through the mess, tangled up with one another like a den of cross-eyed snakes.

"There wasn't even a storefront," said Sunny. "It was in the back of a *bail bondsman's* office."

"What's wrong with bail bondsmen?"

"One of them made a pass at me." She crossed her arms over her chest.

"I'm sorry you had to go through that, Sun." Leathers was down on his hands and knees, sifting through the mess like a kid crawling around under the tree on Christmas morning. "It was the only place I knew that would have all this junk on such short notice."

"You have any idea what you're doing with that junk?"

"I've googled some things." Leathers leaned back and grabbed a stack of printouts off his desk and gave them to her. "Doesn't look too complicated."

"You googled 'how do I rig up my coworker's office with a hidden camera and microphone so I can spy on them'?" she said.

"That's what we're doing, isn't it?"

"I'm surprised you aren't in handcuffs already."

"Google doesn't care what people do. Hey, you know how to use a power drill?"

They didn't get started until late. People had been filing in and out of Sal's office (*my office,* Leathers reminded himself) all day long. Sunny had kept an eye on the situation, sabotaging the mailroom copier with a paperclip so she would have an excuse to cross to the other side of the building and use the one around the corner from the executive suite. The last person Sal had interviewed was at seven that evening, and Sal himself didn't pack up and leave for the day until after eight.

"What the hell is he up to?" said Leathers, when Sunny finally gave him the all-clear. Now more than ever he needed eyes and ears in that room.

Bugging the office started off simply enough. A couple holes drilled near the ceiling in opposing corners of the room, each fitted with a wire with a camera lens the size of a pencil eraser affixed to one end, plus one more hole in the ceiling of Leathers' utility closet where the back ends of the wires ran out and connected to a router that allowed him to switch back and forth between camera feeds on his monitor.

Then the problems began to mount. The microphone was a dud, meaning they could only see, not hear what was happening. Cleanup also took longer than expected. No matter how often he swept the floors and wiped down every surface, Leathers would notice some stray bits of plaster still clinging to the carpet fibers or taunting him from some impossible-to-reach crevice of the radiator.

Worse yet, when he and Sunny finally tested the new setup, they found that the cameras were pointing directly across the room at each other. Half a dozen tweaks – each one requiring them to dodge the overnight cleaning staff as they slipped between offices – made no improvement. No matter how they twisted or turned the cables, they could not get the camera lenses to point downward.

"We need to find a lower access point," said Leathers. "Maybe I can bring this one down, run it through the wall."

"Do you expect Sal won't notice a hole drilled in the middle of his wall?" said Sunny.

"You still have that ficus plant I gave you for National Secretary Day?"

"National Administrative Professionals Day," said Sunny. "And yes, I took it with me when I was banished from my office."

"Go grab it. I've got an idea."

Sunny obeyed with a heavy heart. The ficus was the first gift Leathers had ever given her. An hour later it was in Sal's office, obscuring the hole Leathers had drilled through the back wall. Sunny stood in the middle of the room, her cell phone to her ear, listening to Leathers direct her from the utility closet. She followed his instructions with the doomed visage of an opera heroine.

"Now move back to the door," said Leathers. "Now walk forward. Ok, now sit in the seat there."

"Can you see me?" said Sunny.

"I see you." On the monitor, Sunny appeared as a green, halo-shrouded figure spied through the branches of the ficus, like the target of a Special Ops jungle mission. "We're good to go here. Let's wrap up."

They finished cleaning and arranging everything the way it had been the day before right as the first employees began arriving that morning. Sunny had gone to the cafeteria to get them breakfast while Leathers kept himself glued to the monitor, looking for visual clues as to what Sal was plotting. Several hours in he had yet to spot a pattern. Shortly after Colleen departed, another figure entered and took the seat opposite Sal.

"Now who's that?" said Leathers.

"I thought we tested this," said Sunny. "Didn't you tell me you could see me just fine?"

"I did, but then I knew it was you in there. When you don't know who to expect it's a little tougher to figure out."

"Ugh, it's Sheila," said Sunny.

"How can you tell?"

"The clipboard, for one."

"Oh, there it is, I see it now." Leathers shuddered. "That's one part of the job I don't miss."

****

"It's an educational campaign the Steering Committee and I came up with for OSHA's National Occupational Hazard Awareness Week," said Sheila. She removed a sketchpad from her clipboard and held it up for Sal to see. "'Workplace Safety Begins With U', it's called. Each page has a helpful hint starting with the letter 'U' – Understand Your Surroundings; Use Your Best Judgment; Untimely Reporting of Hazards Leads to Accidents. You get the picture." Sheila snorted and put a hand over her mouth. "*You* get the picture," she repeated.

"Sheila, you're no longer allowed to solicit donations on company property," said Sal.

Sheila's hand remained over her mouth. Sal watched her process the words and saw the moment of recognition reflected in her eyes, which grew to the size of drink coasters. "What?"

"Everyone finds it extremely annoying."

"But…but you can't *do* that!"

"I'm sorry, Sheila."

"You can't!"

"I can. I'm the CEO."

171

"Next week is our brush-a-thon for National Gingivitis Prevention Day!"

"You can have your brush-a-thon, but no more clipboard and no more wandering around the floor asking people for money."

"This is *the Lord's* work!" Sheila hugged her clipboard to her chest. Her shoulders trembled. "Don't you care about your employees' *souls*? True North is supposed to be about spiritual enlightenment. Is it all just dollars and cents to you?"

"I would be happy to work with you on a company-led charity initiative with standardized messaging and an online portal where employees can donate…*if* interested. No more pressure tactics, Sheila. You've been warned."

It took all of Sheila's southern breeding to keep her composure. She stood, curtsied slightly, and offered a dignified, "Good day," to Sal before leaving the room. If there were anything else to discuss she wanted no part of it. Her very identity was under attack. There was no room for compromise.

She could see that insect, Colleen, out of the corner of her eye, grinning as she left the room. This was a conspiracy, plain and simple. A juvenile one at that. Colleen had never liked her, a fact she had made abundantly clear over the years. Sheila didn't care much for Colleen either, but she would never stoop so low as to sabotage her life because of it.

She had always felt more positive toward Sal. He at least had the decency to try to fit in and be part of the team. Or so she had thought. Maybe these were his true colors showing now that he was in power. Well, they had another thing coming if they thought they could get Sheila Pickford to back down that easily.

She was already thinking of ways to fight back as she stomped through the halls, so consumed with strategizing that she didn't notice the gentleman in the overly large cowboy hat or the woman in ill-fitting (*inappropriate, frankly,* thought Sheila) business attire until she had nearly barreled into them.

"I am *so* sorry!" she said, putting a hand to her heart. Her voice regained its sorority chipperness. "I am such a scatterbrain today. I can barely tell if I'm coming or going. Please forgive me."

"Don't be silly, ma'am," said the cowboy, touching the brim of his hat. "Nothing to forgive."

"Can I help you with anything? I don't believe I've seen either of you around here before." Sheila's gaze shifted toward the woman, her smile faltering a bit as she surveyed the acres of exposed skin and seams stretched to the point of submission. *Like a ten-pound sow in a nine-pound sack,* she thought, recalling one of her daddy's sayings. Her eyes lingered for a moment. *More like two-hundred pounds,* she amended.

The woman caught her looking and smirked. "We're new," she drawled.

"That's right," said the cowboy. "First day for both of us."

"My goodness, *welcome* aboard!" said Sheila, with as much southern hospitality as she could muster. She tilted her head and bared two big rows of bleached teeth. *I cannot believe this is who Sal hired,* she thought. It had to be him. Mr. Leathers had his eccentricities, but he was a good businessman and cared about the company. He would never have allowed a pair of carnival acts like these two to be put on the payroll. Then again, he was the one who had let Sal take over. Nothing made sense anymore.

She felt a frown coming on and suppressed it; she would frown later, in private. "Did you receive any paperwork? Do you know where you're supposed to be going?"

"Well now, the gentleman at the front desk told us we were supposed to ask for a *Sheila*," said the cowboy. "You might could show us where we could find her?"

Sheila furrowed her brow. "Yes, I'm Sheila."

A grin spread across the cowboy's face. "I thought that voice sounded familiar. I guess this is for you."

There was no suppressing the gasp that escaped Sheila's throat as a gun barrel appeared in front of her eye, so close she could see down its length all the way to the chamber. It reminded her – ridiculous as it seemed given the circumstances, but no less real for that – of a toy telescope she had owned as a child, the untold hours spent peering out the front window at the goings-on on her street. She imagined looking into the distance, seeing death approach like an unfamiliar car headed toward her driveway. There was no looking away now, no closing the blinds and hiding under her bed.

"*Vamonos*," said the cowboy, jerking his chin.

Sheila turned and stumbled over her clipboard. She hadn't remembered dropping it. "Where...where are we going?" she managed to say.

"First, we're going to find somewhere nice and inconspicuous to hole up. Then, we're going to have us a talk with that boss of yours. You know, the one that don't give refunds."

Sheila gasped. "You!"

"Managed to avoid any buses, I see."

"Be nice, now," said the woman. "She just works here. It's the big boss you want."

"Ain't she a sweetheart?" he said to Sheila. "Now, where's a room where the three of us might have a little privacy. It's time for negotiations to commence."

****

"That woman I told you about is here," said Colleen.

"The one for the conference?" said Sal.

Colleen nodded.

"What's the matter?"

"It's just…" Colleen pressed her lips together, looking down at the floor. "She's dressed a little…*risqué*, is all."

"Ah. Well, it's a different environment, the warehouse, isn't it? Standards are a little looser. She's probably not used to wearing business casual every day. Best not to judge."

"Very magnanimous of you." Colleen sounded unconvinced.

"Can you show her to an empty conference room?"

"She asked if she could speak to you first. Just for a moment."

Sal checked the clock. "I suppose so. It will have to be quick, though, my next meeting is in ten minutes."

"I'll make sure of it," she said, a hint of disapproval in her voice. She stepped out of the office. "Right this way," Sal heard her say.

A second later the door opened, and a woman on the far side of middle age entered. Whatever Sal had been picturing when he'd heard the word 'risqué', the reality involved a lot more woman and a lot less clothing. Maybe warehouses were more different than he realized, he thought. Still, he had meant what he'd said about not judging, and he did his best to keep his mind open and his eyes focused strictly above the neckline.

The woman wore a pleasant smile, but it faltered for a moment once she saw Sal. A curious expression flashed across her face, as if she'd caught a few notes of a song she hadn't heard in years and was trying to remember the name. She quickly got a hold of herself and the smile returned, but Sal could see it was forced this time. Whatever it was that had shaken her up, she was determined to hide it.

"Welcome," said Sal, standing and extending a hand. The woman thanked him as she reached out to accept. The moment their hands touched Sal felt something stirring in the back of his mind. It was not a memory exactly, but there was something familiar about the sensation, as if some long-dormant synapses deep within his brain had suddenly sparked to life again. He gestured for the woman to sit and then followed suit.

"I hope you had a pleasant trip," he said. "Again, let me welcome you to True North headquarters. I'm the chief executive, Salvatore Slocum."

"You're the head honcho?" The woman nodded. "I thought for a moment I'd been pointed in the wrong direction. No offense, mind you. You just seem a little young for the job."

"None taken," said Sal. "I haven't been doing this for very long, to be honest. Until me it had always been Mr. Leathers running things. Burt Leathers, that is. You probably know him?"

She shrugged. "The name rings a bell."

"I understand you're here for the operations conference?"

"You know damn well there ain't no operations conference going on." She studied Sal's face, gauging his reaction, and smiled at what she saw. "What I can't figure out is why you let me come up here anyway."

Sal felt a flutter in his stomach. "I admit I didn't know anything about a conference," he said, carefully. "I just assumed it was something that had been scheduled before I took over, and no one had ever filled me in. You're telling me you made it up?"

"That's about the long and short of it."

"Then I suppose the obvious question for me to ask is why?"

"The short answer is to help a friend. Someone who, like me, has been kicked in the teeth by life a few too many times to bear."

"Ok," said Sal, "and how is this going to help her?"

"Him, actually," said Elmie. "And before we get into the hows and whys, I think I better fill you in on what the situation is. Right now, my friend is at an undisclosed location within these very offices holding one of your employees hostage."

They stared at one another like two poker players who'd gone all in with junk hands. After a few moments Sal reclined a bit, and his face relaxed. "Ah," he said, picking up the phone and dialing a number. Elmie could make out the rings coming through the receiver, as well as the click when someone on the other end finally answered.

"Stefan?" said Sal. "It's Sal. Hey, listen, I know this isn't how these safety drills are supposed to work, but can we possibly postpone this one for a week or so? I get that you're our chief security officer and you have autonomy in these matters, but I'm asking for a favor this time. I understand it's supposed to be random and that real security threats don't care about what we have on our calendars and all that, but I just…look, I really need this. I'm just getting on my feet, and I'm trying to make some big changes here. This is going to screw up my schedule beyond belief."

Stefan, whose mouth had been hovering above his third cup of coffee for the day from the time Sal had started talking, finally took a sip. "I have no idea what you're talking about," he said.

"The drill," said Sal. "The hostage thing."

"What hostage thing?" Stefan set his coffee on the desk. "What are you talking about?"

"The person who's supposedly holding an employee hostage somewhere on the premises."

"Sal, we don't even do simulations like that anymore. It's been more than a year, haven't you noticed? The whole program is under review, ever since they staged that mock Taliban raid over at the elementary school. Legal says it opens us up to too much liability."

"Then what is this woman doing in my office?"

"There's someone in your office right now?"

"Yeah."

"What is she saying?"

"She's saying her friend is holding someone hostage somewhere on this floor! Aren't you listening?"

"Are they armed?"

Sal put his hand over the mouthpiece. "Are you armed?" he said to Elmie.

"My associate has a gun on his person, yes," she said.

Sal put the receiver back to his face. "Yeah, they're armed."

"ACTIVE SHOOTER IN THE BUILDING!!!" screamed Stefan.

Sal winced and pulled the receiver from his ear. "Hello?" he said, a moment later. "Hello?" There was no answer.

A clamor from the hallway made them look toward the window. Outside they could see people running past – just one or two at first, but quickly becoming a stampede that made the floors vibrate from their collective weight. The door opened and Colleen shoved her head inside. "I don't know what's going on! Something about a shooting?"

"There's no shooting," said Sal.

"Not yet anyway," said Elmie.

Sal regarded the woman in front of him with different eyes. His gaze remained fixed on her as he gestured for Colleen to leave the office, which the latter did, reluctantly. "So, you're for real?" he said.

"Very," said Elmie.

"I don't know what happened to your friend, but I have a hard time seeing how this is going to fix things."

"As do I, if I'm being honest."

"Why help him, then?"

"Because people can get pushed to a point where fixing just ain't an option anymore. Maybe that's hard for someone who's running a company when he's still got peach fuzz on his cheeks to understand."

"I understand better than you think."

181

"Yeah? You know hard times?"

"Nothing I'm going to share with you."

"As is your right. You certainly got the bags under your eyes, though I know you corporate types like to burn the midnight oil to show how indispensable you are." Elmie leaned forward. "None of that's here nor there, though. Let's stick to the situation at hand. My friend wants to have a word with you. I'm not here to be his messenger or air his grievances for him. All I need to know is that if I give him the all-clear and he walks himself over here, you won't try to play the hero or call the cops."

"And if I refuse?" said Sal. "This friend of yours is going to start shooting?"

Elmie shrugged. "Most people don't bring a gun into a place like this unless they're willing to use it. I can tell you that's not what he wants, though."

Sal took a deep breath and exhaled. When he spoke again his voice had that strange timbre to it, like a ship's captain exhorting his crew to rally while riding out a gale. "As a man of honor and one who feels deeply the responsibility of his office, I give my solemn oath that your friend will have safe passage to and from this room to levy his grievances against me or the company, be as they may. In return, I demand that he refrain from the commission of any wanton act within these premises, or threat thereof, that may cause harm to any individual in my employ. Should a resolution be found that is acceptable to all, I will do my best to find a way by which I may turn the other cheek and allow those assembled to go their separate ways unharmed. Should it not, well…" He trailed off, staring into the middle distance.

Elmie couldn't focus on Sal's words. She was preoccupied with the hand he had put to his face, right along the side of his nose and mouth, as if he were about to whisper some secret to her across the desk. Nothing he could have said would have mattered in that moment; the gesture spoke loud and clear. It was a message from the distant past, one that for thirty years she hadn't dared allow herself to hope to receive.

****

"Who is this now?" said Leathers. "I can't see her face."

"About the only thing you can't see," said Sunny. "Yeesh!"

"Don't be prudish, Sunny, it doesn't become you." He squinted at the screen. "She is dressed a little loosely for the office, I admit. One of ours? I don't recognize her."

"You don't recognize the person with the greenish blob for a face? I feel like we've already seen them about a dozen times today."

"When did you become so sarcastic?"

"When I spent an entire night helping someone install bootleg surveillance equipment that doesn't let you see or hear anyone."

"Certain sacrifices needed to be made in the name of discretion. This stuff is totally untraceable, you know."

"Of course it is. Who in their right mind would come looking for this junk?"

"All right, all right. Just let me focus."

"Sorry, didn't mean to interrupt your little peep show."

Leathers leaned in closer. "I swear there's something familiar about this woman."

"Been hanging out behind any truck stops lately?"

"Sunny, are you jealous?"

"Of *that*? Ha!" She held her nose in the air. "I just think *some* decorum might be nice. You don't have to stare so hard."

"I'm looking at her face. See there?" He pointed. "When she leans forward like that you can kind of make it out."

"Mm, fascinating." Sunny craned her neck toward the door. "What's that noise? Do you hear that? It sounds like a herd of buffalo running down the hall."

Leathers was too preoccupied to respond. His eyes stayed glued to the monitor while Sunny went to check on the disturbance. It wasn't just that the woman seemed familiar that had Leathers transfixed, it was the way in which she was familiar. No memory surfaced that he could tie her to, not even the ghostly vestiges of a thing long forgotten. This was something from the before-times, before the flash, crashing against the unconquerable divide in his mind again and again like a barbarian storming the gates. He had never felt anything quite like it before. The more he focused on her the greater the sensation became, digging against his skull, as if something living inside were trying to burrow its way out.

"Burt!...BURT!"

Leathers lifted his gaze. Sunny stood in front of him, her face ashen. "There's a shooter in the building!"

"What?" said Leathers.

"That's what the people in the hall were saying. Everyone's evacuating right now."

"It's him. He actually showed." Leathers scrunched up his eyes for a moment, then looked back at the screen.

"We need to go!" said Sunny.

"They aren't moving."

"Who cares?!"

"Don't you find that strange?" He turned toward her again. "There's a shooter in the building, everyone knows about it, and the CEO wasn't warned? Either that or…"

Sunny bounced on the balls of her feet, her hand spinning around like a pinwheel trying to hurry him along. "Or nothing!" she said at last. "Come on, let's get out of here!"

"You go ahead, Sun Bun. I'm staying."

"You can't stay!"

"I put this thing in motion. The least I can do is see it through. Besides, no one will find me hidden away in here." He reached over and put a hand on Sunny's arm. "Go, now. Get outside where it's safe. I'll be with you soon enough."

Sunny looked to the door, then back at Leathers. Finally, she nodded and scampered off, pausing only for a moment to check that the hallway was clear before running for the stairwell as fast as her legs would carry her.

Leathers waited until he was sure she was gone, then turned back to the monitor. The flash of light – that seminal event that marked the start of his existence – played over and over on a loop in his mind. Behind it, an unnamable thing, a shadow calling out to him from across a void whenever he looked at the woman on the screen. That was his real reason for staying, though he wouldn't have expected Sunny or anyone else to understand. He had always trusted his intuition to guide him, and it was telling him now – as emphatically as it had ever delivered any message – that his fate lay in that room.

A vibrating against his leg interrupted Leathers' thoughts. He reached into his pocket and pulled out his True North compass. To his surprise, the glass cover had begun to crack. Inside, the needle spun madly, changing directions like a weathervane in a swirling wind.

Eleven

Sal's first impression of the man holding a gun to Sheila's head was that he looked like a Weeble dressed up as Gene Autry. All that was needed were a few more rhinestones.

"You wanted to talk to me about something?" said Sal.

"I wanted to talk to the man in charge," said the cowboy. "I don't know if that's you or not. You don't look like who I was expecting."

"It's me all right," said Sal. "True North is under new management."

"More's the pity. You picked a bad time to take the reins."

They were gathered together in Sal's office. The woman, whose name Sal still didn't know and who had been watching him for the past several minutes with a sort of barely concealed awe, had moved her chair over. Seated next to her, pale as a tapeworm, was Sheila. Behind Sheila stood the cowboy, pressing the barrel of a snazzy looking revolver into the back of her skull.

"Nice piece," said Sal.

"Glad you like it," said the cowboy.

"I don't like it. I hate guns."

"That's a Colt model 1877 Lightning double action revolver."

"Ok."

"New York engraved."

"Got a name?"

"I call her Berta."

"Not the *gun*. What's your name?"

"Oh." Sal was surprised to see the cowboy blush. "Call me Bagley," he said.

Elmie turned on him. "You moron!"

"What?" said Bagley.

"You gave him your real name?"

"I'm trying to build trust."

"I *trust* you're going to be doing ten to twenty in state lockup when this is over."

"Now, now," said Sal, holding up a hand. "I made a promise. No police, so long as *you* promise to take it easy with that pistol there."

"As you say," said Bagley. "You know why I'm here?"

"Because you want to talk to me," said Sal.

"Yeah, but do you know why I want to talk to you?"

"I kind of figured you'd tell me."

"Oh, I'll tell you all right." He reached beneath his jacket and removed an object, then held it out for Sal to inspect. "You recognize this hunk of junk?"

"The compass?" said Sal.

"It's a compass," said Bagley. "A True North compass. What you sell to desperate half-wits like me."

"Don't be so hard on yourself."

"Look at the needle."

Sal looked. "It's pointing right at you."

"Exactly. No matter where I go it points right at me." Bagley moved in a half-circle to demonstrate. "According to you hucksters that means I've got everything figured out." He gestured around the room. "Does this look like I've got it all figured out?"

"Wait a minute…" Sal looked from Sheila to Bagley and back again. "This is the guy you were telling me about. The one who threatened you because you wouldn't give him a refund?"

Sheila nodded, her eyes round and watery. It was the first time Sal had ever seen her speechless. "Look, don't blame Sheila," he said. "She was just doing what the bosses told her to do."

"That excuse didn't work in Nuremburg, and it won't work here," said Bagley.

"I think fine distinctions can be made between the situations."

"Well and maybe, but don't try and tell me you all don't know you're pushing snake oil here."

Sal held up his hands. "Oh, I admit it. Until recently I was a sales rep. I won't pretend for a minute that I believed anything we were selling was actually going to help anyone. But then, I don't believe in a whole lot. I just said what I said and went on with my life."

"A lot of people out there do believe," said Bagley. "Or crave some peace so badly they'll shell out money for anything that promises to give it, even if they don't believe. I'm not sure which is worse."

"I get it," said Sal. There was a barely perceptible pause, as if he were an MP3 player on whom someone had pressed the 'skip track' button. When he spoke again, it was in the cool, assured tones of an experienced businessman. "At the very least if our company cannot deliver on its promises, then it should have the integrity to admit it failed and compensate its customers. Now that I'm in charge, I can make that happen. No more restrictive return policy. That is my pledge. If customers don't see results, they can return their purchase for a full refund."

He stood and extended a hand across the desk. "On behalf of True North, I would like to apologize for the bad experience you had with our products. We will of course return the money you paid us and would be happy to reimburse you for any costs you incurred while making your way here to our offices."

Bagley looked at Sal's hand like it was a wet dish rag. "It's too late for that," he said.

"What are you talking about?" said Elmie. "I thought that's what you said you wanted."

"Some stiff corporate pleasantries and a handshake? Nah." He glared at Sal like he would at some out-of-towner who'd just wandered through the swinging doors of his favorite saloon. "You might say you get it, but you don't know the first thing about me."

"Why don't you tell me?" said Sal. "But first…let the girl go."

"I'm not on the payroll here. I don't take orders from you."

"Not an order. I'm just saying, you wanted the guy in charge and here he is. I'm obviously not going anywhere. You don't need her anymore."

Bagley considered a moment, then turned to look at his companion. She nodded. "Fair enough," he said. "Out, little lady!" He tapped Sheila on her back with the gun barrel, then gestured with it toward the door.

Sheila stood, pale and trembling still but with a glimmer of hope in her eyes that made her fear all the more palpable. "Thank you, Salvatore," she said. Her voice was strained. "I won't forget this. I promise, no matter what happens here, I am going to do everything in my power to have this year's Polar Plunge dedicated in your honor."

"Get going!" said Bagley. He kept his pistol trained on her as she slipped out the door, then pointed it at Sal.

"You were saying?" said Sal.

Bagley grunted, then moseyed – Sal could think of no better word for it – over to sit in the chair vacated by Sheila. "I was soliloquizing on the subject of hopelessness."

"Is that how you feel?" said Sal. "Hopeless?"

"Ain't nothing to do with feelings. It's the plain and simple truth." He stopped to straighten his jacket. "I may cut a dashing figure, but it's smoke and mirrors. I'm a rotted-out apple with a pristine skin."

"Surely it can't be that bad."

"A man's nothing without a past," said Bagley. "I've been playing a losing hand since the day I was born." While Sal listened in silence, Bagley recounted the same story he'd told Elmie that night in the motel, from his successive adoptions throughout childhood to his lack of human connection to his perpetual attempts at self-improvement. By the time he was finished he sagged in his chair like a parade balloon with a busted helium tank.

"I'm really sorry," said Sal. "I know it's hard…"

"You don't know a thing," Bagley muttered.

"About being adopted? I know enough. My own parents gave me up when I was just a little kid."

A sharp gasp made them turn their heads. Elmie sat with both hands over her mouth. Her eyes were the size of golf balls.

"You ok, Elmie?" said Bagley.

She nodded. "I…yeah. I…um…I was just thinking of something. I…" She trailed off, too distracted to care that Bagley had spoken her real name.

Bagley turned his attention back to Sal. "How old were you?"

"When they gave me up? I don't know exactly. A year, year-and-a-half, maybe? No more than two."

"You don't remember your parents either?"

Sal shook his head.

"Hmph. You know, under different circumstances I'd probably be buying you a drink right about now."

"I'd settle for you not shooting me."

"No promises." Bagley sighed and used his finger to trace the embroidery on his shirt. "Still, look at you. You're young yet, running a company, probably got a nice girl waiting for you at home…"

"Used to," said Sal. "She left."

"Ain't that the way?" said Bagley. "I can't imagine a man in your position will have much trouble finding another, though. And what have I got? Gray in my whiskers and a couple hundred bucks in a savings account. What woman's going to want that?"

"What about her?" said Sal. He looked at Elmie. "Sorry, I just assumed the two of you were an item."

Elmie opened her mouth to respond, but no words came out. She looked at Bagley, who blinked vacantly as he shifted his attention between her and Sal. Together they resembled a pair of goldfish trying to make sense of the new tank into which they had just been introduced.

"I just figured," Sal continued, speaking to Elmie, "there must be something there for you to stick by him through all of this."

"Yes…" she said, after a pause, "there is something." But what, she thought? There must be some attraction there. She had latched onto Bagley like a puppy from the moment she'd run into him at the bar. What was it that had drawn her to him? He wasn't what you would call a handsome man, though he wasn't half as bad looking as he seemed to think. Pity? Certainly, she felt sorry for Bagley, even sympathetic. Here was another of life's losers, a label she had no hesitation applying to herself as well. It was that shared feeling of being stepped on, a couple pieces of gum on the bottom of life's shoe, that had made her go from wanting to kill Bagley to sitting by his side now as he held a corporate executive at gunpoint. Held her *son* at gunpoint.

She was lonely. That was the truth of it. She had been lonely ever since the moment she had signed the papers giving up custody of James Jr. to the State. It was a feeling fully incorporated into her sense of self, as intrinsic to her as her height or weight. It would always be a part of her, she knew, because she had accepted that she would never see her son again. And now here he was all these years later, sitting right in front of her – a stranger, a fully grown man, yet still the same toddler she remembered giving tearful kisses in the lobby of the Department of Children and Families building that awful day thirty years ago.

The calculus had changed. She could see now the outlines of a future for herself, one where she was whole again. How she would navigate from this moment to that imagined future – one where her son forgave her and was a part of her life – was a problem to be solved later. The important thing was that it was now possible. All she needed to do at this moment was convince Bagley to walk away. There was nothing more to be gained here, nothing left to prove. Could she love Bagley if it helped her get her son back? She thought she could. She looked across at him and smiled.

Bagley had run out of steam. From the time he had left his home, throughout his travels across the country, right up through his present-day infiltration of True North's offices, he had maintained the unwavering conviction – fueled by resentment and adrenaline – that his cause was a righteous one. He had known, in his heart of hearts, exactly what he needed to do to make things right. Now he wasn't so sure. His plan had worked. He had gotten his apology. He had gotten his refund, even some extra money to boot. Yet he felt nothing. Worse than that, in fact – he felt embarrassed, like an unruly airline passenger screaming at the flight attendants for more pretzels, only to realize as he's handed his extra bag that all the other passengers are staring at him in disgust. He had made himself the center of attention, and he didn't know what to do with it. He wasn't used to people caring about what he had to say.

Elmie was smiling at him. He should have stayed at the Alamo that night, waited there for her till she came back from the restroom and seen where the evening took them. It was some kind of miracle that she'd managed to track him down, that despite his shabby treatment of her she was here now, still sticking up for him. What more could he ask for? He had a job. He had a place of his own – not much of one, but he doubted Elmie was the type to turn up her nose at wood paneling and a foldout couch. What did he care whether the world respected him? He could walk out of here, start a new life with a beautiful woman. All he needed was for the young man across the desk to show a bit of mercy and allow him to slink away with his tail between his legs. His face softened as he returned Elmie's smile. Then he turned to Sal, tamping down the trepidation that spread through him like a brushfire while trying to maintain the fiction that he was in charge.

Sal couldn't make sense of it. Somehow, he had managed to gain control of the situation. Despite the fact that his thoughts hadn't strayed from "*I'm going to die*" from the moment Bagley had entered the room with his revolver, he had managed to keep talking, and it appeared his words were having an effect. Maybe this was another leadership quality Leathers had secretly managed to impart to him. *Leathers,* he thought. It should have been him here, contemplating his mortality. He was the skinflint who had implemented the no-returns policy. Hell, he was the one who had made his fortune selling broken compasses to the needy and vulnerable to begin with. However flattered Sal had been by being chosen as Leathers' successor, whatever latent vanity it had tickled, it meant nothing to him now. For the moment, survival was sufficient. Hopes and dreams could wait.

He looked Bagley in the eye, weighing his words carefully. "You're right, our stories aren't identical. But in a fundamental way we're the same, you and I. We fear being abandoned more than anything, more than death.

"When my girlfriend left me, I was crushed. I may, as you said, find someone new and move on with my life, but I can tell you that when I came home that evening and saw the note from LuAnn telling me she was never coming back I instantly became a little boy again, small and frightened without a single protector in the world. It's a type of loneliness – helplessness, really – most people can't understand. But you and I do.

"Whatever other advantages I may have been blessed with, one thing you have that I don't is a partner." Sal counted off a beat and then turned to Elmie, keeping to the script he'd fashioned in his head. He was surprised to see tears forming in the corners of her eyes. "Someone who stayed when times were at their hardest." He turned back to Bagley. "You may find this difficult to believe, but I envy you. You've found a thing that – I've learned – neither money nor status can buy – loyalty. From the bottom of my heart, I am sorry for what this company did to you. Anything I can do to make things right, to ensure the two of you find happiness together, I give you my solemn promise to see that it's done."

There was more Sal had planned to say, but seeing the effect his words were having he decided to cut it short. Bagley's shoulders sagged. He exhaled, a long, drawn-out hiss, as if a lifetime's worth of demons were being exorcised through his nostrils. He slipped the gun beneath his jacket, then turned and extended a hand across the divide toward Elmie, who was dabbing at her cheeks with a tissue. Her gaze lingered on Sal for a moment. Then she set the tissue aside, leaned toward Bagley as if drawn by a magnet, and reached out with both hands to envelop his. They stayed that way for several minutes, gazing at one another in adoring silence. Bagley reached with his free hand to brush a strand of hair from Elmie's face, letting his fingers run over the top of her ear and down the back of her neck.

Then the door flew open.

A tall, skinny man with a shock of wavy hair standing on end burst into the room.

"YOU!" said Bagley. He pulled out the revolver.

Elmie leapt to her feet. "J…Jim?!!"

"Elmie!" said Leathers, staggering toward her as if he'd just awakened from a hundred-year slumber. "I remember…!"

The next sound any of them heard was Elmie's body collapsing onto the floor.

Twelve

"Elmie? Elmie, wake up!"

Leathers crouched over the fallen woman, one hand cradling her head while he patted her cheek with the other, trying to revive her. Sal watched his efforts play out through the crook of Bagley's arm. No sooner had Leathers appeared than the cowboy had darted behind the desk to wrap Sal in a headlock, pressing the pistol tight against his temple.

"You get away from her!" said Bagley. "Back on up, hear?"

Leathers paid no attention. He grabbed Elmie's hand and clutched it tightly, massaging it with his thumb.

"Hands off my woman!" said Bagley.

Sal flinched. Every time Bagley yelled, he pressed the barrel of the Colt even harder against the side of Sal's face. The cold metal bit into his skin. He could imagine the circular indentation that would be there when the gun was finally taken away. *If* it was taken away. He gritted his teeth and did his best not to complain. Better an indentation than a gaping hole, he thought.

A moaning could be heard from down on the floor. Elmie's eyelids began to flutter. "Jim?" she said, blinking. Her breathing grew faster as she started coming to. "Is it really you?"

"It's me, Elmie. I'm here…"

"I feel lightheaded. I'm all shaky, like I'm vibrating from the inside out or something."

"Don't worry, I'm with you now. I'll take care of you."

A sound like a thunderclap made them clutch their ears. When the ringing stopped, they all looked at Bagley, smoke oozing from the barrel of his pistol as he pointed it at the ceiling. "*Attencion*!" he said.

"You doofus!" said Leathers. "What the hell is the matter with you?"

"Don't give me any lip, hoss, you least of all. You're that huckster that looks like a carrot from the TV commercial. I've been meaning to have a word with you."

"I know exactly why you're here," said Leathers.

"Yeah?" said Bagley. "I bet you do. Is that why you sent this poor kid out to front for you? Hired yourself a human shield?"

Leathers said nothing. Bagley shook his head. "Not only a liar, but lily-livered to boot."

"We can trade insults later," said Leathers. "Elmie needs our help."

"How do you know her name?"

"Jim…" said Elmie, woozily. "Jim, why did you leave us? Why didn't you say anything?"

"Hold on a minute." Bagley's eyes narrowed. "Jim? *Your* Jim? The one who disappeared on you?"

Leathers ignored Bagley as he eased Elmie into a sitting position, turning her so her back was propped up against the radiator. He crouched close by and peered into her eyes. "Elmie, are you ok? Tell me what you're feeling."

"Sick," she said. "Like I'm going to puke." Sweat beaded up across her face. Her breathing was shallow, ragged. Every exhalation brought with it a rattling sound, as if her lungs were filled with BBs.

"I'll bet she is," said Bagley. "You got some nerve waltzing in here playing the hero thirty years after you vamoosed."

"Shut up, I tell you!" Leathers snapped over his shoulder. "There's no time for that right now!" He looked back at Elmie. "Listen to me…I didn't know what had happened. There was a flash. I woke up in the middle of the woods, and I couldn't remember a thing – where I was, who I was. I know how it sounds, but…"

"We all know how it sounds," sneered Bagley. "When Elmie told me about what had happened to her I wondered what sort of creep could do something like that to such a fine woman. And his own child, to boot! Now that I know it was you it makes perfect sense.

Mister Enlightenment himself." He shook his head. "You look like a celery stalk."

"I thought you said I looked like a carrot," said Leathers.

"Take your pick. I don't much care for vegetables."

"It shows."

"What's that supposed to mean?"

"It's a comment on your general appearance."

"At least it don't take me thirty years to appear in the first place."

"Stop it, both of you!" said Elmie. Her eyes grew maudlin. "I believe you, Jim. Really, I do."

Leathers sighed with relief. Bagley, on the other hand, made a face like he had just been served a plate of root vegetables for dinner. "Elmie, you can't possibly believe this cock-and-bull story."

"There was a storm that night," she said. "A bad one, lots of lightning. It's possible."

"Possible?" said Bagley. "Come on, Elmie! The man sells magic compasses for a living. You're going to take *his* word for it?"

"The compass isn't magic," said Leathers. "It merely detects the change within the individual. *Give me your lantern and compass, give me a map, so I may find my way to the sacred mountain.*"

"Don't go quotin' Psalms at me."

"You know your scripture, eh? That's all True North is, my cowpoke friend. A set of tools to guide one to the mountain."

"Yeah, sure it is. That's why my compass always points at me, cause I've reached the mountaintop." Bagley dug in his pocket, took out his compass and tossed it onto the desk. The needle swung in his direction. "There you go, Elmie. That's the man who's asking you to take him at his word. A shyster, telling people like you and me he can fix all our problems for fifty bucks we can't afford to spend." He addressed Leathers directly. "All I wanted this entire time was my money back and an apology. An admission that none of this stuff is real."

"It is real," said Leathers. "No matter what you say."

"Jim," said Elmie. Leathers could see the look of reproach in her eyes. However much she wanted to believe him, her trust had its limits. He couldn't blame her. Words could only do so much. He needed to show her.

Leathers stood and faced Bagley. He held his hands at shoulder-height and took a step toward the desk.

"Easy now," said Bagley.

Leathers nodded and continued his slow advance. When he had cleared half the distance between them, he jerked his chin and lowered his gaze toward the compass. Bagley, though, was already looking there, his attention drawn by the needle as it trembled and shifted its focus back and forth ever so slightly, like an old bloodhound that can no longer trust its own nose. Bagley, as if in sympathy, felt a vibration somewhere deep in his stomach. Indigestion, he wondered? He had barely eaten anything all day.

Step by step, Leathers made his way to within arm's reach of the desk. Bagley moved back a couple paces, dragging Sal along with him. Suddenly, the compass's needle spun decisively away from Bagley, no longer wavering but centered precisely on Leathers. To drive home the point, Leathers slid over to the left a few feet, then did the same thing to the right. Both times the needle followed as if connected to him by a string.

"What in blazes?" said Bagley.

Leathers looked up and met Bagley's eyes. "You see? Not a hoax. Your journey just has a ways to go yet."

"Save it," said Bagley, but with less conviction. The vibration in his stomach had grown more intense. It reminded him of when he'd jammed a fork into one of the wall sockets at the orphanage as a kid. He could feel it now rippling out to the surface of his skin and working its way down his arms. "I don't know what your angle is, but I suggest you get back before I put a plug through this kid's skull."

"NO!" cried Elmie. "Don, please…"

"Dammit Elmie, don't let this phony get to you," said Bagley. "I know you loved him once, but he ain't the same man he once was."

"That's my son!" she said, pointing.

"What?" said Bagley.

"Um…" said Sal.

"Junior?" said Leathers. He looked back and forth between Sal and Elmie. Suddenly, it all made sense – the vague feeling of recognition he had felt, the compulsion to choose Sal to succeed him over all the other possible candidates. It was an echo of himself he had spied in that young man's face.

A thought occurred to him, and he shuddered. He had put his son in harm's way, offered him up as a sacrifice in his own stead. Had he known who Sal was at the time he would never have done such a thing. Only now he did know. Ignorance was no longer a defense. There was only one thing to do.

"Cowboy," said Leathers. "Let him go, and you can have me. I won't put up a fight."

"Please, Don," begged Elmie. "Listen to him."

Bagley looked like someone who realized he had just objected at the wrong wedding; his feelings hadn't changed, he just wasn't sure anymore where he should be directing them. "If you're asking, Elmie, then ok." He turned to Leathers. "How do I know this ain't some trick?"

"You tell me what to do and I'll do it," said Leathers.

"Turn around," said Bagley. "Back to me, hands out at your side. Now, kneel."

Leathers carried out Bagley's instructions to the letter. Once Leathers was on his knees, Bagley placed the barrel of his gun to Sal's back and slowly removed the arm from around his neck. "Ok, now," said Bagley. "You go on over there, nice and easy, and take a seat beside your mama. No sudden movements, hear?"

Sal tiptoed around the desk and past Elmie, ignoring her maternal looks as he picked out a spot several feet away to take a seat. Whatever she was feeling at that moment he wanted no part in reciprocating.

"Now you," said Bagley, speaking to Leathers again. "Back on your feet, nice and slow. Know that my Colt's pointed right at you, ready to sever your spine."

"I understand," said Leathers, serenely. When he was on his feet again, Bagley ordered him to walk backwards until he was beside the desk. Bagley then reached out and grabbed the back of his shirt collar, giving him a shake as he pressed the barrel against the base of Leathers' skull.

"Careful!" said Elmie.

"Don't worry," said Leathers. "He's not going to hurt me."

"You so sure about that?" said Bagley. Already, he could feel the vibrating sensation from before returning. His muscles twitched, as if a second brain were trying to take control of his body.

"Don't antagonize him, Jim!" said Elmie.

"He's not a killer," Leathers said to her. "I'll be fine."

"Don't talk about me like I'm not in the room," growled Bagley. The twitching was growing worse. He shifted his weight from one foot to the other and felt his knees almost buckle.

"You don't have to do this, Don," said Elmie. "You said you wanted an apology, that you wanted someone to listen and take you seriously, that's all."

"As if an apology from him would mean anything." Bagley coughed. He could feel his throat starting to seize up. He leaned his flank against the side of the desk for stability.

"Anything I say to him would ring hollow, he's right," said Leathers. "He needs to find acceptance within himself."

"Quit talking like I ain't here!" said Bagley, coughing again. A chill passed through him, and he shuddered. For the first time he noticed he was covered in sweat. It appeared, seemingly, all at once, enveloping him from head to toe like a shroud.

"Jim, please stop pushing his buttons!" said Elmie.

"I'm just saying what I know to be true. It can be hard learning to be ok with all the pieces of oneself…"

"Shut it!" growled Bagley. He was wheezing now. Flecks of spit rained from his mouth to sprinkle across the desktop.

"We see a beautiful painting in front of us, yet we fixate on the fly that's crawling across the canvas…"

"He's quotin' them goddamn cards!" said Bagley. He felt as though his skull were lined with red-hot needles, plunging over and over into his brain. A dull pressure made his eyes bulge, straining at the confines of their sockets.

"For every minute a man is angry, he loses sixty seconds of happiness…"

"That ain't wisdom…you're just converting units of time…" All at once, Bagley's symptoms began to recede. The vibrations grew fainter and less frequent, like the vestigial ripples of water from a stone that has sunk to the bottom of a pond. The burning and pressure in his head began to ease.

"Don't start your day with the broken pieces of yesterday. Every day is a fresh start. Every day is a new beginning. Every morning that we wake up is the first day of our new life…"

Bagley felt his eyelids droop. The world had gone fuzzy around the edges. He had never noticed that before. Was his vision starting to go, he wondered? It might be time to look into glasses. He coughed, a dry, rasping eruption from deep within his chest that rattled his body, yet sounded strangely muted to his ears. Was his hearing failing as well? One indignity after another. Things decay day after day and we race to fix them, he thought, patching holes in a boat we know is destined to sink.

"Don't give into fear. Every situation is temporary. There is something good in every bad day…"

Up ahead, Bagley could see a bed of pine boughs arranged just off the side of the road. He couldn't believe his luck. It seemed as though he'd been walking for as long as he could remember. Daylight had long since faded; the night was dark, no moon in sight. He would set up camp here, bed down for a while. He moved to the road's edge, then reached out to grasp the branch of a nearby tree to steady himself. His fingers encircled the smooth bark, and he squeezed…

"Trust yourself," said Leathers. "The answers are there, inside you. You've survived a lot and you will survive whatever is coming…"

There was a *'bang!'*, and a red sunburst painted itself across the ceiling. Someone screamed. A moment later, both Leathers and Bagley slumped lifeless to the floor.

When the police and paramedics arrived on the scene, they determined that Burt Leathers had died from a single gunshot wound to the back of the head. Don Bagley, meanwhile, had suffered cardiac arrest. Something, most likely some sort of magnet, had caused his pacemaker to turn itself off.

Thirteen

The funeral for James Meadows, aka Burt Leathers, was held one week later in his hometown of Plumville, Arkansas, population 1,737. At times it seemed as if twice that many people were in attendance, not just locals eager to remember a beloved member of the community who had once been thought lost forever, but also a significant number of True North devotees from all over the country.

They had begun arriving in ones and twos almost immediately after the service was announced, forming a makeshift camp on the outskirts of town that quickly took on the look and feel of a traveling circus. Their backgrounds were varied, but all credited True North with changing the trajectory of their lives. Many considered Leathers something akin to a spiritual leader. Such was the strangeness and fervency of their beliefs that the service was moved from First Baptist Church, where the Meadows family had for generations been members, to the Unitarian Chapel out near the township line. The Baptists couldn't say for sure whether it was a sin to bring compasses into a church, but they figured there was no sense in taking chances.

Old Pastor Hymes, who had presided over Jim's baptism as a boy, was dispatched to lead the service. At ninety-five years of age, he feared Godly retribution as little as the judgment of his fellow man. Jim Meadows would mark the forty-third individual he had shepherded from baptism to the grave. "Dunk 'em in the river, then dump 'em in the dirt," as he liked to put it. Whatever theological quandaries the current funeral might have posed for the rest of his clergy, they did not trouble Hymes. "Unitarians make great coffee," he said, upon accepting the invitation.

There would be no 'dumping in the dirt' this time, however, as Jim's – that is, Leathers' – will had specified that he wished to be cremated. As it was, the service was conducted with an urn at the front of the congregation instead of a casket, a rare bit of novelty for a ritual that, in Plumville, remained largely unchanged year after year. Even stranger, at one point the proceedings were put on hold so that a procession of True North customers could stand before the urn, one at a time, to say a few words about the dearly departed. Most opted for a quote from the True North instructional manual or daily affirmation cards. Pastor Hymes welcomed this development, as his sermons had grown increasingly short over the years. "I don't have it in me to do a full set anymore," he explained. "It's nice to have a supporting act."

Once the service had concluded, the assembled gathered outside so that Leathers' ashes could be "scattered to the North", as it was worded in his will.

The responsibility for said scattering fell to Sunny, his longtime assistant. In her flowing, black Versace dress and oversized sunglasses she made a striking widow – or would have, everyone agreed, if Leathers had ever gotten around to making an honest woman out of her. As she exited the chapel, clutching the urn to her chest, a breeze tousled her hair and made her skirt billow about her ankles, like Dicksee's *Miranda*.

With so many compasses present finding which direction north lay was no difficulty. Unfortunately for Sunny, the breeze continued unabated as she unscrewed the lid from the urn and gave the ashes a heave. Their northward trajectory quickly took on a south-southwesterly aspect. Only Sunny's cat-like reflexes spared her a rather morbid final coupling with her former lover, but more than one attendee would later confide that they suspected a piece of Burt Leathers had come home with them that day. As for whether or not they had succeeded in honoring Leathers' wishes, it was eventually agreed that what they had witnessed was a message from beyond, a lesson that while others can get you started on your journey the rest is up to you. Had he not checked out of this world already, Bagley would have died laughing at that one.

Having left no last will and testament and with no next of kin, Don Bagley's body had been destined for the crematorium at the Boynton County morgue.

However, a last-minute intercession from Elmie secured a burial plot just outside the boundaries of the Dog Iron Ranch in Oologah, Oklahoma, birthplace of Will Rogers. She imagined he would have liked that, being laid to rest beside the pastures where the great vaudevillian learned the skills that would one day make him a trick roper with Texas Jack's Wild West Circus. It took nearly every last penny of Elmie's savings to make the arrangements, but it was worth it to help assuage the guilt she felt over not talking Bagley out of his hare-brained plot sooner.

There was little Elmie needed the money for anyway, confined as she was to county lockup as she awaited trial. Prosecutors had planned to charge her with Accessory to Murder, Unlawful Detention, and several other felony offenses, but mitigating evidence provided by Sal convinced them that a plea deal was an acceptable alternative in her case. She would spend two years in state prison, followed by another two years of supervised probation, but after that her life would be hers again. Whether or not Sal would continue to be a part of it was something he would need to think about in the interim.

As Leathers had died without voiding Sal's contract, Sal became the sole owner and chief executive of True North, LLC. Whether this constituted a happy development or not was settled conclusively when a Federal Trade Commission subpoena arrived requesting documentation related to their "investigation into True North's deceptive trade practices". Luckily for Sal, it did not take long for the FTC to uncover that the company's myriad problems had not been properly disclosed to him before he was put in control, and that the contract naming him as Interim CEO was defective on its face.

Indeed, so scathing was the section of the FTC's report detailing the contract's deficiencies that Stilton Farnsworth quoted from it verbatim throughout his argument before the State Supreme Court, offering it as clear evidence of his ineptitude as an attorney. The court agreed, ordering Harvard Law to pay Stilton significant compensatory damages for "an education that has proved deleterious not only to the man, but all of humankind". Unfortunately for Stilton, the FTC's investigation also uncovered that he had "knowingly drafted the contract for the purpose of placing Salvatore Slocum in a position likely to result in bodily harm or death", and much of his monetary award had already been spent mounting a defense against possible criminal charges.

Largely penniless and with her husband now unemployed, Graciela Sandoval – no longer Grace Sanders, whether Stilton approved or not – leaned in fully to her newly stoked feminist fury. As details of Elmie Duncan's arrest and life story began coming to light, Graciela recalled that afternoon on the median strip when she had spotted the woman and her now-deceased partner stalking down the sidewalk on their way – she now knew – to True North's offices. She felt an immediate kinship with Ms. Duncan, seeing in her a woman led astray by unscrupulous men and suffering unjustly for their actions. With minimal embellishment she was able to parlay her near run-in with Elmie into a successful grant application, providing her with the funding necessary to construct a conceptual art installation casting Elmie as a modern representation of the scorned woman/mother figure.

As for the company itself, True North was soon seized by the federal government and liquidated. Each employee (Sal included, now that he had been demoted back to sales rep) was provided with two weeks' severance pay and a complimentary True North kit as compensation. It was a curious sight to behold that final day, as hundreds of office drones milled about on the sidewalk in front of 17 Industry Way staring down not at their phones but at compasses, hoping to glean some insight into what they should do with their lives.

"Look at us," said Sal. He stood in a cluster with Colleen and Sheila near the edge of the group. "We're like lemmings. Our company was just outed as a fraud, and here we are consulting their stupid compasses like they're some sort of oracle."

"You've got yours out," said Colleen.

"Yes, and I'm an idiot," said Sal. "I think the last week has proven that."

"I don't know," said Sheila. "It makes sense, in a way."

"What's sensible about any of this?"

"It's hard when you know you're going to wake up tomorrow with no idea what you're supposed to be doing. Do you know what you're going to do?"

"Not really," he admitted.

Sheila nodded. "Until today all of us had a routine – we knew where to go, what time we needed to be there, and what to do. That's gone now. I could put a positive spin on it and say that this is the best thing that ever happened to us, that now we're free to pursue whatever it is we think will bring us happiness, but we all know that's a lie. Only people with money enjoy freedom. For everyone else it's just scrabbling around trying to find a rock to grab onto before your head sinks beneath the water."

"I've never heard you so grim," said Sal.

"It's scary, is all." She shrugged. "I suppose anything that provides a sense of direction, even if it's as silly as this compass, takes some of the pressure off."

"What is your compass telling you?" said Colleen.

"That I'm facing east," said Sheila. "Maybe that's it. I've never been to the east coast before. What do you think, a small-town, southern girl in the big city? What could go wrong?"

"Mine says I'm facing southwest," said Sal.

"Ooh, the lonesome, dusty plains."

"You sound like that Bagley guy. Still, I guess it's as good as anywhere else. There's nothing keeping me here anymore."

"What are you going to do out there in the desert?" said Colleen.

"I don't know," said Sal. "Something different, whatever it ends up being. The only thing I'm certain about is that it's time for a change."

****

"Hello, Dave Smith? This is Salvatore Slocum calling from Blue Mesa Insurance. I hope you're having a nice day. Are you busy at the moment?

"Please don't hang up! I just...I've noticed that you recently purchased a new riding lawnmower. Congratulations! How do I know that? Well, our company maintains many valuable partnerships in both the retail and financial services sectors, which allows us to better identify individuals such as yourself who could benefit from the products we offer.

"For instance, wouldn't you love to ensure that the lawnmower you just purchased will still be there for you, giving your grass that perfect cut ten, or even twenty years from now? Unfortunately, even the best-engineered appliances succumb to wear and tear, and accidents will always happen, as I'm sure you know. What's that? How am I sure? Well, that's life, right? Murphy's Law – what can go wrong will? You see where I'm coming from. You don't? Let me explain…

"As the nation's foremost insurer of landscaping equipment, we know a thing or two about yard-tastrophes. Pardon? That's a term the company coined – catastrophes that happen in the yard. Fair enough, sir. Like I said, it's the company's term, not mine. But let's say, for example, one of your little ones leaves his jacks lying around in the grass. You don't see them, you run them over, and next thing you know you've got a shrapnel bomb under your mower's deck. What? Yes, I know it's not the 1950s. Yes, I *know* you don't play jacks on grass, it was just an illustrative example.

"Look, when you bought your mower you probably purchased a service plan through the retailer, am I right? That will cover you for, what – one, two years? It's like they structure those plans specifically so they'll expire right before you start seeing any problems in your equipment. The beauty of Blue Mesa is, we'll be there for you when you need us. You're correct, sir, that is also one of our corporate slogans.

"Sir, I don't want to beat around the bush. You seem like a perfect candidate for one of our premier policies. As I mentioned before, our company [*give them the clear big picture value and benefits of your product specifically aimed at solving their obstacles*]. [*Provide examples of how our company differentiates itself from…*]"

Sal heard a click on the other end of the phone. "Hello?" he said. "*Hello?* Dammit."

"You read the prompt out loud," said Colleen, craning her neck around the wall of Sal's cubicle.

"I know." He sighed and pressed the button to hang up. "Who buys insurance for their lawnmower, anyway?"

"Probably someone pretty neurotic. Or with expensive tastes in mowers." She chuckled to herself. "Don't you think it's funny to headquarter a lawnmower insurance company in Arizona?"

"I'm sorry I dragged you into this, Colleen."

"You didn't *drag me into this*, I asked to come. I have a mind of my own, you know."

"I know, I know." Sal wheeled his chair back a few paces and turned to face her. "I guess I shouldn't complain. I don't know what I expected, letting a compass plan out my life."

"It's not so bad. The bosses don't seem to care whether we sell anything or not. And the scripts are kind of funny. I especially like the one where we tell them that 'we know you care about your lawn the way you care about your children'."

"One guy actually agreed with me," said Sal. "It was depressing."

"Is there anything I can do to cheer you up?" said Colleen.

"Ask me a question."

"Ok...would you rather live on a tropical island but have no arms or legs, or have all your limbs but live alone at the South Pole?"

"Right now?" said Sal. "Either one sounds like paradise."